Young Writers

COMPETITION ... OLS

TALES

From Merseyside

Edited by Laura Rogers

Disclaimer

Young Writers has maintained every effort
to publish stories that will not cause offence.

Any stories, events or activities relating to individuals
should be read as fictional pieces and not construed
as real-life character portrayal.

YoungWriters
First published in Great Britain in 2005 by:
Young Writers
Remus House
Coltsfoot Drive
Peterborough
PE2 9JX
Telephone: 01733 890066
Website: www.youngwriters.co.uk

SB ISBN 1 84602 226 6

Foreword

Young Writers was established in 1991 and has been passionately devoted to the promotion of reading and writing in children and young adults ever since. The quest continues today. *Young Writers* remains as committed to engendering the fostering of burgeoning poetic and literary talent as ever.

This year, *Young Writers* are happy to present a dynamic and entertaining new selection of the best creative writing from a talented and diverse cross section of some of the most accomplished secondary school writers around. Entrants were presented with four inspirational and challenging themes.

'Myths And Legends' gave pupils the opportunity to adapt long-established tales from mythology (whether Greek, Roman, Arthurian or more conventional eg The Loch Ness Monster) to their own style.

'A Day In The Life Of ...' offered pupils the chance to depict twenty-four hours in the lives of literally anyone they could imagine. A hugely imaginative wealth of entries were received encompassing days in the lives of everyone from the top media celebrities to historical figures like Henry VIII or a typical soldier from the First World War.

Finally 'Short Stories', in contrast, offered no limit other than the author's own imagination while 'Hold The Front Page' provided the ideal opportunity to challenge the entrants' journalistic skills, asking them to provide a newspaper or magazine article on any subject of their choice.

T.A.L.E.S. From Merseyside is ultimately a collection we feel sure you will love, featuring as it does the work of the best young authors writing today.

Contents

The Creative Writing

The Sacred Orb

'I'm just visiting the river!' Kiera shouted racing down the steep hill. Kiera was thirteen, she had brown hair, stunning eyes, rosy lips and an enchanting smile. She believed in all magical creatures.

Kiera's hillside cottage stood above a rippling river. Every day she went to skim her finger across the surface, imagining living beneath it. Suddenly, an unknown force dragged her into the water, she felt as cold as ice.

Opening her eyes she saw before her four water nymphs with thin bodies and pointed ears, in every hue of blue.

Around them the coral shimmered in all colours of the rainbow and the light danced upon them.

'I'm Lavender, please help us!' she pleaded, 'we need to retrieve our sacred orb otherwise we become human!'

The other three nymphs stood silently.

'Of course!' whispered Kiera.

'Thank you!' they chorused.

'Take the necklace,' said Lavender, 'it'll warp you to the orb.'

Suddenly Kiera materialised in a dark place scattered with pointed rocks. The orb glowed purple in the dim light. It was guarded by an angry looking nymph, whose face was like thunder. She waited for him to fall asleep and silently she removed the orb from its pedestal. Using the necklace she was suddenly standing in front of Lavender and the other nymphs.

'Thank you,' they exclaimed, their eyes twinkling like stars. Kiera felt a jolt and found herself back beside the river. She wondered whether she would ever see the nymphs again ...

Samantha Bresnahan (12)
All Saints Catholic High School

Surviving The Tsunami

On Boxing Day 2004 disaster struck in the Indian Ocean, an underwater earthquake erupted and sent a huge wave to southern India, Sri Lanka, Thailand and Indonesia.

The wave was going 400mph and swept away everyone and everything in its path. The wave caused more damage than 1,000 atomic bombs.

Lots of homes were destroyed and more than 150,000 people have died and the figure is still. rising. England and lots of other countries are donating money and campaigning and the English government have so far given £60 million. Food has stopped getting to poor villages because of roads collapsing and an aeroplane crashing on the runway, but now it has moved and aid is still trying to get through. Also people are living on the streets and there are so many orphans and refugees.

When you walk past all you can see is all that was left of buildings and houses and rubbish all over the floor. This paradise has turned into a rubbing-ridden graveyard. A man tried to save his little baby but it was too late, the man said, 'I wrapped him a sheet. He was frozen.'

I said, 'You're frozen you poor little man, you're frozen.' I got him into a rickshaw and I was rocking him and I just started wailing. Many more people have lost their lives in this disaster. It's terrible.

Kayleigh Goodwin
All Saints Catholic High School

The Tenth Sense

Ciara was turning thirteen on Friday 13th of December, it was in three days.

She was really looking forward to it. Not because she'd get presents and money, it was because she'd receive her power. The tenth sense.

The tenth sense was a power like no other. She would be able to see all around the world. She would be able to hear everything going on in the world, when she wanted to. She would be able to smell, feel and taste everything in the world. It was a power like no other and it was hers.

When the day came she was really happy, she was dead excited. Her mum Jayna would teach her how to use the powers and would guide her till she was ready to use them, without her mum.

On that day she got her Book of Shadows, which was a rule book and guide to use her powers. It was made especially for her with her name on which would have to be kept safe.

Her life was already great, but now it was so much better having *The Tenth Sense*.

Laura Bennett (12)
All Saints Catholic High School

A Day In The Life Of Hermione Granger

I'd always liked the Harry Potter books and films and always wondered what Hogwarts would be like. Then it happened.

It was a Tuesday, the alarm on my watch went off as usual, 7am. I opened my eyes, I was surrounded by white curtains. This wasn't my bed! I pulled them back to discover four other beds in the room, with sleeping girls in them. Then I realised where I was, in Hogwarts! I looked at the chair beside me. Lying on it was a uniform. I put it on and went downstairs. I was in the common room. Was it real?

I sat on a chair by the fire when I heard voices. It was Ron and Harry. I couldn't believe it!

'Morning Hermione,' said Harry cheerfully, 'you coming to breakfast?'

'Yeah,' I replied. I couldn't wait to see the great hall. I looked at my body, I was Hermione.

Breakfast was delicious. Bacon, eggs, beans, the lot. After breakfast we had transfiguration with Professor McGonagall, divination with Professor Trelawney and double potions with Snape. Very enjoyable, except potions. I then went sightseeing, then to charms with Professor Flitwick. It was then lunchtime!

That was delicious too, shepherds' pie. After lunch we had the rest of the day off for homework. I sat down to my potions essay when I fell asleep! I woke in my own bed to find I'd fallen asleep reading. It wasn't a Harry Potter book. It was a potions book ...

Hayley Johnson (12)
All Saints Catholic High School

Bully Bruce And Jim!

Once there was a boy called Jim, he was lovely, he was always good at everything, even maths.

One bright sunny morning when Jim was walking down the road, through the dark woods and across the wide road and on to school, bully Bruce came along.

Bruce was the most horrible boy in the world. He walked over to Jim and kicked him in the shin and he put him against the wall and said ... 'Give me your money now or else.'

As bully Bruce was doing this to Jim, Mr Bernard saw it, he was an old man of course, but he walked over to him and at the top of his voice he said, 'Pick on someone your own size!'

Big bully Bruce never picked on Jim or anyone again and every time he saw Jim he ran away.

Kerry Lace
All Saints Catholic High School

The Unhappy Girl

One day there was a little girl called Sindy and there were two nasty girls who didn't like her at all. Their names were Suzanna and Reanna, they always wanted to make her life hell!

One Monday morning, Sindy was walking to school when she saw Suzanna with a big bucket of syrup, and Reanna with a box of feathers, so Sindy hid in the trees and when they had gone she ran home and told her mother that she wanted to go and live with her nan, her mum said it was okay. So she packed her bags and started to walk through the forest but Suzanna and Reanna saw her and followed her.

Five hours later Sindy got to her nan's and then Suzanna and Reanna said, 'We are sorry Sindy for picking on you for all this time.'

Sindy said, 'It's OK, I forgive you.'

They all went to Sindy's nan's house and had some tea, then they were all friends again.

Amy Castell (11)
All Saints Catholic High School

A Day In Life As A Footballer's Wife

A typical day in life as a footballer's wife would be exciting, glamorous, lots of media interest, but most of all, expensive.

Footballers' wives would wake up early, spend loads of time getting dressed and then either get together with other wives or spend time on their own. But it is not all about spending. If they have children it is their responsibility to occupy them and take them places. When they do, the press are always there.

Footballers' wives are all over the magazines and news if they are snapped. If they do have any spare time they don't waste it watching TV, they go to their husbands' football matches and support them.

Footballers' wives' weight loss is a big thing. It is not always glamorous being a footballer's wife, because their husband goes to dinner parties and always has other women after him. Women then talk to the papers the next day and say that they had a date with the husband.

Some people are very cruel, they think they can get money out of footballers all the time, and it really hurts their wives.

It is not all glamorous being a footballer's wife, they have their good times and bad times.

OK, they have got the money, nice clothes and fame, but they also have all the hassles.

When I grow up I would not like to be a footballer's wife, never knowing where he is going to be. I would like to marry a loving man and have children.

Laura McCarthy (11)
All Saints Catholic High School

Ghost Story

Hello, I'm Sophie, let's travel back to when I was 9, which is now about five years ago. Sit back, relax and I will share my story with you.

It all happened when I was on holiday in Spain. Oh, it was beautiful, it had massive palm trees, banana trees, any fruit you named, it was on a tree!

On my second day I was playing with a little boy I had met, we decided we would explore the real Spain and get to know it a bit better.

We passed lots of things like shops, game arcades, clubs, cycles and loads more.

After a while we got fed up so we went back to my hotel.

Hanging on, before I tell you any more, let me tell you about my friend who I was with. Well, his name was Matthew, he was quite loud, he had blue eyes and blond hair. He loved football, he supported Everton.

Now then, where was I up to? Oh yes, know, when I got back to my hotel, just as we'd reached the second floor ... *slam!* A door was opening and shutting as if it was trying to make a signal.

We walked over a bit further to the door. Matty saw cobwebs, spiders and lots of scary things. I was frightened so I shouted, 'No, don't go in, please no!'

Matty replied, 'No you come in, I find these things really interesting! Come on, I am going inside,' Matty whispered.

'No,' I spluttered.

Before I knew it I was in a very dark and gloomy room. I was shaken, I didn't like this ...

'Boo!' shouted something.

I tried to run but Matty grabbed me and spoke quietly, 'It's OK.' Next a whistling sound came, even Matty felt scared now. Maybe it was just the floor or the wind, but whatever it was, it was *scary.*

'I'm friendly, will you run if I come out?' yelled a voice.

'Yes,' I screamed.

'Hang on, no, no come out we won't run,' Matty yelped (you could tell he was scared really).

Before I could move ... a white body, with a green face and no legs came out. 'Hello,' it murmured, but before it could saying anything else we ran out.

We ran as fast as cheetahs to my door, number 72, we got two big padlocks without any keys, then we put the padlocks on the door with the weird creature inside, so that it couldn't get out, and since then we decided to keep it a secret till this day.

Bobbie Forshaw
All Saints Catholic High School

A Day In The Life Of Space

Boom! went the newly made rocket.

'I've made it!' shouted Lindsey. She was so happy, she was jumping out of her shoes. But also a bit nervous. Well, it would only be the next day and she would be into space.

The next day Lindsay went to NASA to fly to space. The time came, as all the hours had passed. She thought about all the safety, hazards and rules. Then she heard the loudspeaker shouting for Lindsey to get ready for take-off.

As Lindsey made her way towards the rocket, she met up with her crew. It was time to leave Earth. As she clambered into the rocket which was her favourite colour, blue and had funny decorations on it ... *5, 4, 3, 2, 1, lift-off!*

Off she went, up to space, soon she was in space and all she could see was the shining stars. In the distance Lindsey could see something, that to her eye was a moon. So she decided to take a closer look.

An hour later the crew were getting ready to land on the moon. Then, as they took a step onto the moon, they didn't know what to say, they were all star-struck. As the safety cord spread out further and further around, Lindsey started catching sight of the Earth. It was a beautiful sight under the very dusty moon. Also Lindsey had spotted the red-hot, fiery ball. It looked like the sun! It was time to come home now. As Lindsey was on her way back to Earth she wrote a little poem called *Life In Space.*

L iving
I n space
F or
E ver

I nteresting
N o life

S pectacular
P ace
A stonishing
C unning
E xcellent

As she arrived home Lindsey couldn't wait till she could tell everyone about her amazing stories and adventures. As the crew landed the craft they were all tired.

Lindsey Hill
All Saints Catholic High School

A Day In The Life Of The Chick-A-Dee Flea

I should think that most of you readers know what a flea is: those teeny, tiny, creepy-crawlies that live in 'awkward places' on the bodies of humans and animals. Your cat may have had fleas, your dog, hamster, your rabbit, or your mouse, or even your grandma! You may have even had the dreaded pests living in that cosy nest on the top of that head of yours. Fleas are everywhere, but one type of flea remains a mystery to all of human kind. A flea so small and discreet, yet very mischievous and a real pain in the neck. The type of flea that comes and goes whenever and wherever it pleases; the Chick-a-Dee flea.

Chick-a-Dee fleas can be found living in peace throughout many homes around the world; from China to Luxembourg, and of course, your very own bedroom. Those creaks and crunches you hear echoing through your house in the middle of the night are most likely to be whole armies of Chick-a-Dee fleas marching from room to room. All the while searching for the ideal pillowcase, mattress or duvet that can be turned into a safe night-time habitat.

However, the Chick-a-Dee flea's regime doesn't stop there. The fleas are as busy during the day, as they are during the night. When morning breaks and it is time for you to wake up and prepare for the oncoming day, Chick-a-Dee fleas emerge from their beds, too. They cling tightly to the small hairs on your arms and are carried wherever you go. At first, they wait dormant and unnoticed, in the hope that an opportunity will arise ... the opportunity to catch you unawares ...

The most likely place for a Chick-a-Dee flea to strike is in a public situation such as in a classroom, a shopping centre, a car park, inside a crowded lift, or even when you are with your boyfriend or girlfriend.

Whenever you find yourself in such an environment, a Chick-a-Dee flea can sense this by using heat signals sent through your body temperature and through the hairs on your arms. This is their cue to do what parasites do best, *irritate!*

Without you even knowing, the Chick-a-Dee fleas instantly scatter themselves over your body at lightning speed. Eventually they make themselves dizzy and need to rest. When they do, they decide that wherever they stop, to lie on their stomachs and roll around in unsteady circles. In turn, causing you to itch. Now this is all very well, if say, they stopped on your neck, or your ear, or your chin for example. But what happens when they stop in those 'awkward places' that were mentioned earlier on? I'll tell you what. They don't stop to give you any thought; they just roll, and roll, and run, and roll. Soon, the effects start to take their toll. But what are you to do? So many eyes are watching your every move and at the same time, the irritation grows worse. Soon it gets unbearable, you can't hold back for longer, all you can do is ...
'Eeeuuurrrrggghhh! You are so disgusting!'
... Scratch.

After the moment has passed, the fleas quickly return to the hairs on your arm (which are now snug and warm as a a result of your embarrassed, blushing skin). Here is where they stay until you return home, unless of course they are agitated again and decide to go for another little sprint. When you finally return to your bed again at night, the fleas retire back to their homes and sleep the night away. Or, they may leave in their armies once again and travel through your house in search of a new residence.

And there you have it; the day in the life of a creature that you didn't know existed, even though it plays a very important part in the many fowl-ups that take place throughout life. If one day from now, you should feel the discomfort of the demented frenzy of the Chick-a-Dee flea, keep in mind these two words: 'Oh dear' ...

And that's putting them mildly!

Katy Osborne (13)
All Saints Catholic High School

Wind Trespasses School

Top set students at All Saints were horrified at the gust that blew their hair back.

One week yesterday at All Saints School, a terrible gust of wind blew away people's hopes and dreams. It started with the wind, then ended in the rain.

Teachers and students of the school sobbed for hours.

Could this be the start of a disaster?

Cold abomination

Last week at All Saints School children waited patiently for the sun to come out, but that's when tears started.

Who could have known that one measly gust of wind could change smiles into sobs? We asked Miss Gallagar, what really happened? 'It was horrible, no one knew what was going to happen, it came out of nowhere. I can tell this devastation will be upon us for a while.'

Jahllisha Lindsay (13)
All Saints Catholic High School

The Day That Spun The UK

Homes, lives and the UK devastated.

An unexpected hurricane hit the coast of England on the 22nd June at 1.34pm. Homes, lives and the UK were left devastated. The hurricane hit the UK after days of glorious sunshine. The weather was predicted to stay like that but it was only when the sky turned grey that we knew something was wrong. 'Rain poured down and thunder and lightning broke out in the sky, before we knew it a hurricane hit the beach, so we ran for our lives,' David Knight, a witness of the tragedy said.

'People were told to take shelter but some thought it was just an ordinary weather storm, one of these was my wife,' Tony Bush, a life left with no future.

The tropical storm hit the UK at 74mph. The hurricane was formed in the Atlantic Ocean and brought torrential rains, high winds, incredible waves and storm surges.

After this terrible storm, beaches were left flooded and cars, trees and buildings were destroyed

Many people were on the beaches, this area was the worse place to be during this type of storm. Because of no warnings people were not told to stay away from the coastlines.

After the storm people were left trapped under rubble. The only thing people could do was to search for missing bodies of lost members of families or friends.

'My fiancé and our expected baby were swallowed by this terrifying storm,' Nick Bailey lost a future family to this destroying menace.

'Yesterday we were happy until nature shocked us all,' said John Moore.

Sarah Burke (12)
Birkenhead High School

Drink Driver

Drunken coach driver has killed 17!

Children lost their lives today while driving along the M62 on the way to Speke Hall. The driver of the happy ALS coach, Thomas Mooney was thought to have been drink-diving while taking a class of Year four children from Liscard Primary to the beautiful mansion. 17 children and 2 adults have died and others have received minor injuries.

The drunken driver, Thomas Mooney has recently gone through a divorce and is extremely upset. His friends say, 'Ever since he has been divorced he has been drinking. We are extremely sorry for those people that have lost their family. A very shocked child who survived said, 'It was all a bit of a blur, all I can remember is that I was sitting at the front talking to my friend and there was a loud beep and my teacher stood up straight away. She reached over him and started shaking him. He was asleep. The next thing we are in a ditch and everyone is bleeding. There was glass all over me. I had never been so scared, I had a shiver right the way down my spine.'

A parent of a child that has died said, 'I have just lost my child all because one stupid man can't handle his divorce Thomas' ex wife said, 'I didn't realise how much the divorce had upset him, I am extremely sorry. I'm sure if Thomas was alive he would feel very guilty, there is a lot of heartache and I hope some families will recover.'

Hannah Gilmore (12)
Birkenhead High School

When He Went On Holiday

Young Thomas Green found out his parents had booked a holiday to Florida and he would get to go to Disneyland and meet Mickey Mouse.

The next day at school he told his best friend James Hunter. James had already been to Disneyland and told Thomas all the best places to go. Thomas told Miss Showers his teacher and she said she wished she could come, she laughed and said she could hide in his suitcase, Thomas laughed at this.

He went home and asked his mum how long it would be till they went.

'Only two weeks away,' she said, 'and your brother Sam is coming home from university.'

At school James had brought some maps of the Disney Parks. There were lots of parts like Magic Kingdom and Blizzard Beach. The two weeks passed slowly but surely, until the doorbell rang and it was Sam back from university. He was also very, very excited. He had been on the internet and got lots of information on Disneyland.

They all went to bed early to get up early. Thomas was the first up that morning, he woke Sam and his mum and dad. They had booked a taxi for 7am and it was already 6.30am.

They got up and had some toast and Dad had his coffee. When the rather large taxi pulled up and beeped its horn, they loaded the boot and they all piled in, then they were off on the holiday of a lifetime.

Jennifer Dowling (12)
Birkenhead High School

Train Crash Disaster

Children's lives were lost when the local Bebington train crashed into a ditch!

Children's lives were lost on the train going on their school trip because of an unfinished track. The train driver was to blame for he knew it wasn't safe, but decided to take a risk without informing anyone. Eighteen lives were lost and only ten were saved with serious injuries. The school teachers and assistants were all unable to help the dying and injured, but eleven-year-old Percy Andrews saved the day by contacting the Emergency Services.

Percy has received a medal from the police and fire brigade. The train driver is held in the police station being questioned. The paramedics were lucky to get the survivors out since there were piles of rocks and heavy materials layered on the train, not giving access for the paramedic team to get though. Many of the parents agree on taking their children back to school for a special service in remembrance of the children and teachers who were killed in the accident. The local trains from Spital to Birkenhead will not be in use because of the accident and repairs will take place straight away. The council are writing a formal letter to those who were involved in the accident and are receiving compensation. At two o'clock today there will be a minute's silence for those who died in the accident and those who were injured.

This article is in remembrance of the train crash.

Emma Dodd (12)
Birkenhead High School

A Day In The Life Of Kelly

In a tomb far away the corpse of Kelly hid in the cobwebs and dust. Let me tell you of her past and why she died so young. She had secrets she tried to hide but found it hard when her family were in need.

One day in the town of Lincoln, Kelly was sitting under the old oak tree giving remedies to the sick and elderly. Her treatments and tonics were famous throughout the land. Many people would come from all around to get treatment from her. But one day when the merchants came she caught the eye of young Boric. From that day Boric stayed in the village with Kelly and soon asked her to marry him.

Boric told Kelly that he couldn't marry her until they had told each other their secrets. So Boric told Kelly that he and his family had stolen from the king's knights and when the king found out his father was hung and quartered.

'I would never tell anyone else about that, so I trust that you will keep my secret and that you will now tell me yours,' whispered Boric.

Kelly took a large breath and whispered, 'I'm a witch.'

Boric ran to the mayor's cottage and told him of Kelly's secret. The mayor went to the cottage where Kelly was hiding; he grabbed her by the arm and dragged her into the centre of the town ...

Abigail Dawson (12)
Birkenhead High School

Harry And The Pigeon

Once upon a time there was a little worm called Harry who liked to look at the sun through his sunglasses. One day he emerged from his little hole and stared at the sun for a whole hour. When he got back into his holey home, everything went dark. He was blind. His mother scolded him and his father locked him away for being such a naughty worm!

He was disabled now and couldn't go to the special Worm University his father had put his name down for. So he was sentenced to a lifetime of sitting in his room, eating the mud his mother passed under the door.

Then after a whole year of not emerging from his room, he cracked. He absolutely had to get out! So he crawled out and up and poked his head through the soft, damp mud into the nice blazing sunshine. He felt the cool breeze, then without a warning a pigeon flew down and bit his head off. His parents were devastated.

The pigeon flew over the farm and urinated. The yellow splodge landed on the farmer's new tractor. The farmer pulled out his rifle and shot the pigeon. Mrs Farmer later cooked it in a pie and Mr Farmer choked to death. The man doing the post-mortem explained to Mrs Farmer that her husband had choked on a very small, very geeky pair of sunglasses.

Sally Wexsteen (14)
Birkenhead High School

The Dragon Sun

In the beginning there was darkness. Earth was still. Humans moved slowly and quietly. The dragons were bored. Their planet, Endrigon, sailed through space and came to rest near Earth.

The dragons saw how depressing it was to live in a place of darkness and decided to intervene. Their almighty leader was an enormous monster of a dragon. His scales were blood-red and they shone like burnished gold. His heart was warm as fire and felt sorry for us pitiful humans. He decided to stay on Earth and light our lives, but he alone could not light the Earth.

He was Torrido.

The great dragon council held a meeting. Eventually a decision was reached. The dragons stood up tall, forming an enormous circle and began to sing. Dragons' singing is a wonderful thing. They are like the legendary angels, but far sweeter. Torrido stood in the centre and towered over them, his eyes golden. They wove their individual songs, but each contained this verse:

May your golden glow seek out the sky
May humans never wonder why
And when you look through space and time
May the wind whisper our rhyme
Torrido

The last word sparked the ring into fire. It reached up into the sky and enveloped Torrido. He gave a roar, and sweeping his leathery wings, took off. He seemed to burn a hole in the sky, plummeting towards Earth. He caught himself and swept around, sending light scurrying into the Earth. The dragons were satisfied.

Steffi Webster (13)
Birkenhead High School

A Day In The Life Of ...

I sat bolt-upright, my eyes straining from a bright light. Mum must have switched the light on to wake me up. But it wasn't a school day, was it?

Where was my bedroom? In place of all my possessions there was a four-poster bed, a lit show-biz mirror and an open door with a rainbow of shoes glistening from the door frame.

'Cassidy!' a voice shouted. There was a knock at my door.

'Come in.' A woman burst through the door.

'Cass, what are you doing? You're going on stage in ...' she glanced at her watch, 'precisely one hour and thirty-three minutes. Now get ready.'

On stage? Why would I be going on stage? I looked at the clock on the wall next to me. Thirteen minutes past five! That was the longest lie-in I have ever had, although I was still tired. Another woman came through the door and placed an arrangement of roses on the cabinet. There was a note attached to one of the stems. I reached out to reach it, 'Dear Cassy, I love your music and really enjoyed your show last night. Your voice is truly amazing. Lots of love, your greatest fan, Jennifer Lopez.

J-Lo! J-Lo knows me. Wow, I must be famous to be about to perform and have Jennifer Lopez practically worshipping me. I was a celebrity. This was going to be the best day of my life.

Laura Mackey (13)
Birkenhead High School

Why Me?

'Lucy, get here now!' my father roared.

I rushed down the stairs in panic. I knew I was in trouble. I was in deep trouble. I stood at the bottom of the stairs awaiting my fate. He beckoned me and cautiously I obeyed. His huge fist flew through the air and my jaw clicked out of place as it connected. His other fist closely followed and thumped my stomach. I lost my footing and the room spun as I flew through the air. Then a searing pain shot through my head as it hit the wall and darkness overcame me. What had I done to deserve this? Why was this happening?

I awoke in a hospital bed connected to a drip, an oxygen mask strapped to my face. A few minutes later my mum walked in, tears in her eyes. She smiled, trying to mask her sadness, but I could see right through it.

Once I had been there watching her in the same pain I was now in. I tried talking to her, but my jaw wouldn't move. I tried again and a searing pain shot through my mouth. Tears flooded my eyes, what had he done to me?

A sudden hatred of my father surged through me. I hated him, why was he so cruel?

A policeman walked in and told us of my father's arrest. He would never be able to harm us again. I'd lived my life in fear of him, now I was safe.

Rhiannan Lay (14)
Birkenhead High School

Faith

'Yes, Mrs Oak, I'll prune the dogroses,' shouted Chuck towards the house. Walking towards the stagnant overgrown pond, he looked at the beautiful old house with its porches and balconies.

'I would love to own a house like this, but it's not really a house, more like a secluded heaven out here.' Later he had supper and a wash and traipsed up to bed.

Chuck was woken up at 3am by a baby crying. He thought he was dreaming. He went downstairs to have a scout around. He saw an old basket ... 'Oh my gosh, it's a baby!' He took the little girl up to his apartment; he would keep her there till morning when he would tell Mrs Oak.

Two weeks later, Chuck still hadn't told anyone about his adopted baby, but that afternoon Mrs Oak came to him and asked him flat out, 'So what have you named the baby?'

Chuck couldn't believe his ears but replied, 'Her name is Faith.'

'Oh what a precious name! I've had a baby, she's sixty now, I was only twenty when I had her. She was beautiful, Grace I named her. My mother never knew of her. I lived away you see, in New York. My husband got called for the army and later died. So it was me and Grace alone. Promise me one thing young man, never leave your baby, because I know how much a little girl needs her daddy.'

Sarah Langford (14)
Birkenhead High School

All Alone

The crunching of the leaves under my feet seemed to get louder and louder as I walked through the murky forest. I felt alone and scared. I could hear the twittering birds nestling down to sleep, while I pondered the forest.

I wish my mum and dad would find me, why did I take this dare? It's so silly, maybe if I started shouting then someone would find me.

'Help, help, Mum, Dad, find me please!' I want to go home, I can't endure it. *I've got to get out of here as quickly as possible,* I thought and ran. I don't know where to, I just followed my feet.

Not long after, I'm sure I heard the sound of traffic. I started yelling, '*Mum I'm here.'* I could see a light. My heart was leaping for joy, *Oh please Mum let it be you.*

Broken branches were stabbing into my legs as I ran. My eyes started to play tricks on me and everything went black. I started to scream. I felt I was going crazy. I fell into a pool of mud and just lay there and began to cry. I was cold and lost. The sun was starting to rise now, the light was creeping up behind me trying to peak through the trees to see my washed-out face. Suddenly I felt a huge grip around me. It was my dad. I had been found!

Rachael Hughes (14)
Birkenhead High School

Lily

'Lily, wake up now please.' Lily opened her eyes, they were dark blue like the ocean. She slowly sat up, her long golden hair was perfect. She stood up revealing a perfect figure. After dressing she made her way down the large spiral staircase. Maids rushed around to help her, she brushed them away, then she heard the sound of large paws. Through instinct she spun around, her long white dress followed her. A huge black dog skidded into her feet, glad to see her. When she entered the kitchen her mother was already sitting at the table. 'Darling, why don't you wear your tiara, aren't you proud you're a princess? Go and put it on after breakfast. And really, Prince William is coming to collect you soon; you do remember you are going out with him today don't you?'

'But Mother, I am going out with my friends today.'

'Oh no you're not, go upstairs and get ready.'

Ten minutes later the doorbell rang and there was a knock at Lily's door. 'Princess, it's the door for you.'

Lily went downstairs yet again. She curtseyed and he bowed awkwardly. He took her hand and led her to the horse-drawn carriage. As they were going down a bumpy lane a man threw himself in front of it. The horses reared, the carriage fell to its side and they both stumbled to get out of the way. The prince yelled with pain.

Lily looked around in horror!

Francesca Gibson (14)
Birkenhead High School

Beyond The Pond

As I stood and gazed at the large weeping willow tree I couldn't help but think how spectacular it was. Its great branches draped over its colossal trunk with extreme dignity. Its fine elegant leaves flying in the wind like a multitude of tiny kites. Its tips gently rippled the shimmering pond.

The sight softened me as it was so glorious. It was a splendid day, the sun's rays were very intense, yet the chilling breeze was extremely refreshing.

The pond looked so chilled, I desperately wanted to splash around in the pearly pool, dunk my dry head under the freezing cold water and fling my long soaking wet hair over my shoulders.

The willow's huge trunk seemed to have many fantastic images of animals, people and fairies. The tree looked so exciting, I decided to climb it. I wrapped my short thin legs around its huge trunk and holding onto a weedy branch I heaved myself up. From there on it was easy. I weaved myself in and out of the swaying branches making sure they didn't snap.

The gigantic tree was so enormously tall that it took me over an hour to climb. Once at the top the view was spectacular.

The pond went on for miles and beyond that there was another world altogether. It was the city life, cars and motorbikes zoomed past each other, beeping their extremely loud horns. I thought to myself, *one day I will venture out into the world, beyond the pond.*

Emma Fearnley (14)
Birkenhead High School

Freedom

'Colin James Hughes will be hanged at 10 o'clock for threatening the President of the United States.' Silence fell in court.

'Take this man away.'

Colin tried to break the grip of the guard. He yelled, 'I am just an ordinary man, fighting for freedom. How can the colour of my skin make me so different from you?'

His voice echoed in my ears. My husband, my love, my life, was being taken from me. All I could do was bottle up my fears. I ran from the court, I needed to say goodbye. I attempted to shout, there was a large lump in my throat. A watery film clouded my vision. I wiped my eyes but Colin was gone.

I stood alone, ice gripped my heart. I faced the platform where my husband would be slaughtered. Crowds gathered, laughing as they grouped. The daunting doors were flung open and Colin was pushed out. They roared, my stomach lurched. How could they be so cruel? I couldn't keep silent.

'I love you Colin, be strong.'

'Lily, don't leave me,' he replied.

'I will always love you. Remember, one day we will be free.' The river of tears flowed again. 'I'm so proud of you, remember that,' I exclaimed. I heard him cry as his head was placed inside the rope, I heard him sing, how his voice warmed my heart. The crowd became silent as the clock struck the 10 chimes, on the 10th he yelled ... *'Freedom!'*

Stephanie Edge (14)
Birkenhead High School

In The Cornfield ...

She ran and ran. The fields seemed endless. The corn clung onto her as she grazed past it as if it would never let go. Her eyes were focused on getting home but the darkness covered her like a shroud making it impossible to keep calm. The steep, slippery track of the field suddenly took a sharp turn and she lost her balance. She fell into the corn and looked up as they towered over her and seemed to exchange quick glances about her.

As quickly as she fell she was up again and running as before. What happened earlier had to be forgotten. Her clothes were torn and her body battered and bruised. The salty bead of a tear rolled down her already wet cheek and held onto the skin, frozen and lifeless. She dared to turn round and saw him fast approaching behind her. He wasn't running like her but had a quick walk. She picked up her pace and still looking behind her ran deeper into the field.

She came to another unexpected turn and again lost her balance. As she lay there her legs turned to jelly and she couldn't get up. He was coming. She began to retreat backwards into the stems of the corn. They stood stiffly and left her unable to escape. He was above her. All memories came flooding back. He knelt down to her, stroked her damp cheek and as he whispered in her ear she closed her eyes ... waiting.

Kirsty Dalton (13)
Birkenhead High School

A Day In The Life Of A Princess

As I woke up I stared around my room. The sun was shining through my silk curtains, I got out of my bed and looked out of my window. The garden looked wonderful, the water from the fountain trickled and glistened in the sun.

I walked over to my dressing table and slowly began to brush my hair, I then walked to my wardrobe and put on my pink gown and gloves, for the final touch I added my tiara with jewels encrusted on its shimmering silver surface. I began walking down the staircase to the grand hall, my dress flowing like a stream behind me. I reached the great hall, my maids came rushing over to me asking me thousands of questions. I had had enough. I sent them all away and walked through the stained glass patio doors into the garden. The garden was so tranquil and beautiful. I could hear the birds singing so sweetly in the trees. There were so many different types and colours of flowers it was like a rainbow.

My maid Bridgette came out to find me. 'Bridgette, I am ready, this is what I shall wear.' Bridgette nodded and left. I hated it when people were always following me and asking me thousands of questions.

I left the garden and entered the great hall. Bridgette was talking to a man I had never seen before. His hair was brown and his blue eyes glistened. I thought to myself, *I'm in love.*

Victoria Crosthwaite (14)
Birkenhead High School

My Day As A Dog

The pleasant smell of a new day was in the air. I could hear the vague footsteps of Lucy, stumbling down the stairway. She ambled through the lounge and into my humble abode. There I was, crammed in and encased between my blankets. I was all homely and snug in my bed and before I had even pondered it, I was out of it and dashing towards her like a bullet from a gun. She greeted me warmly and put me outside. I hadn't been outside long before I got called.

'*Tilly* ... walkies!' I dashed towards the door. We were off! I loved going to the beach. It was a chance to be naughty and get mucky at the same time. I really enjoyed my walk, splashing in the water was great fun. I was back in the car later and off back home. Uh oh, I could hear the faint noise of taps running upstairs - this meant bath time!

'Come on Tilly,' Dad said, as he swooped me off my paws. Up the stairs I went and I was plonked into the bath. I was scrubbed from head to toe in Tresemmé shampoo. Dad turned around, so I *shook!* Water flew everywhere! 'Oh Tilly!'

I had just started to get used to a nice warm bath, when I was hauled out and swaddled in a towel. I was taken downstairs and I lazed in front of the fire. Off to bed it was for me.

I ambled to my bed to be tucked in by Lucy. Another thoroughly enjoyable day.

Lucy Cox (13)
Birkenhead High School

What Will Become

The lofty stone wall towered over me, its coat of moist, matted moss hauled over its colossal frame. The marshland surrounding me engulfed my feet and the outlying land was perishing, the icy atmosphere penetrating my fiery soul. It was tugging at my heart, tightly gripping it in its violent clasp. The eerie moon's reflection bounced off the diminutive, dingy and hazy pond. At first, mystery chased me, eager to embrace me, but soon, the barren land ruffled me, worry and concern flooded me. The withered trees glared, watched over me, snagging at my hair, silvery-grey in colour from the midnight's light, as their gnarled branches wove a taut barrier around the desolate field.

I was now a prisoner; I knew there was no escape. My only company was the occasional whistle of the wind whispering to the substantial clouds parted by the moon's strength. My memories before I came here were slowly dripping away, filtering through my mind, which was progressively losing the battle against the elite army of fear. Soon, it would be swarming with repulsive and obnoxious thoughts, evil taking over good! I slowly awaited my nightmare to cease, yet I received the opposite. The sinister and threatening night adorned me in a thick yet bitter and arctic coat of fear, the chilling ambience draining me of warm blood and joyous emotions. All that was left was an empty body, deprived of its soul, my mind overrun by the power of insecurity and terror.

Lucy Beer (13)
Birkenhead High School

Same Misery, Different Happiness

The Earth's population is expanding! Currently there are approximately six billion people living in this seemingly big, but small world.

There are so many people, and we are all so different. We all have our different quirks, habits, hobbies, appearances and ethnic backgrounds.

If we were all the same, with the same feelings, reactions and motivations then the world would have no diversity. There would be no such things as elections, and there wouldn't be a Prime Minister, because we would all be the same.

We would all have the same views on education or none at all, and there may not be teachers because it would be like they were teaching themselves years ago. So the population wouldn't be so bright. If you think about it, everyone would want the same job, the same pay and even live in the same country.

If everyone had the same job, this would be a tragedy, as we need lots of different jobs to keep the world populating, and the land growing.

Lastly, if everyone was the same it would be utterly hard to reproduce. So therefore I conclude we would definitely not exist being the same.

In the world we live in now, sometimes people can find it hard, living in the skin they are in, and may hate being different.

I feel that we should all be celebrating, because everyone who is living at this precise moment, is keeping the world going by simply living, hopefully loving, dreaming, and reaching for the stars.

Holly Wright (13)
Birkenhead High School

A Day In The Life Of A Science Lab

Another day at Krothington Hall. Mrs Mothball came into set up the first lesson of the day.

They might be doing something with fire as it is the middle of winter. It's raining and the heating doesn't working in the lab. I've just remembered it's 4G this morning. They are not concentrating on the safety instructions.

Boom! There we go. Tom McCormick seems to have created a volcano and got what seems to be horse manure and leaf mould compost all over himself. There goes the bell. Detention starts now. What will we be doing next lesson? Hopefully some more things to do with fire. Huh, plants and 5D. Photosynthesis and all that jazz. Ah the sweet smell of toast and tea as 5D come into the classroom with their break. Cactus plants today, a lot of writing. While eating their toast, I can see an accident waiting to happen. What do you know, instead of drinking her tea, Kate Severed has managed to drink the beer that they were doing an experiment with in class. I know why all the class are laughing, but they are not looking at Kate, they're looking at the teacher. She seems to be fighting a giant fly trap with a rolled up science textbook. She has bruised it pretty bad and I think she has won. Now for my nap, no more science lessons till after lunch.

Francesca Wray (13)
Birkenhead High School

A Day In The Life Of . . .

This prison is cold, filthy and dark. I have arrived at Holloway Prison and I am now ordered to take off my clothes. This is a dreadful indignity for me. I am used to having my hair tied neatly back and a fashionable hat on my head. I shiver into some old, patched and stained underclothes in the shelter of a bathroom. I pull on some coarse brown woollen stockings with red stripes and a hideous prison dress. I fish a pair of shoes out of a basket filled with old and odd shoes. I am given coarse sheets, a towel, a mug of cold cocoa, hard bread and shown to my cell. It is my first stay in prison, but I know it won't be my last.

My name is Emmeline Pankhurst and I am a suffragette, campaigning for women's votes. I am the head of the WSPU (Woman's Social and Political Union). We started our crusade peacefully enough using words to try and convey our message to Parliament. However, we did not get anywhere so we have been forced to turn to violence. Yesterday, March 2nd 1912, I, along with hundreds of other women, swarmed through the West End. We had armed ourselves with stones and hammers and together caused thousands of pounds worth of damage by smashing windows and starting fires. Along with two comrades, I also threw bricks at the Prime Minister's house. To succeed in winning the vote we need 'deeds not words'. Alas, for yesterday's deeds I am rewarded with incarnation. However, within my heart, I know this battle will eventually be won.

Harriet Wilson (12)
Birkenhead High School

A Morning In The Life Of The Queen

It was 4am in the morning and I felt a cold wind blow over me. I looked around and I was in a strange room. It was approximately four times the size of my bedroom and beautifully decorated. It had pink walls with dark brown beams across the ceiling. I was lying on a king-sized four-poster bed with purple gauze curtains draped around me. My quilt was made of pink silk from Syria with pale pink daisies delicately embroidered on. I got out of bed and there was a purple silk dressing gown and white fluffy slippers waiting for me. I put them on and wandered cautiously out of my room.

As I looked out, I thought I was dreaming. I was in the main hall. The floor was made of beautiful white-pink marble and there was a golden chandelier hanging from the roof. I walked to the dining room where there was a table full of delicious food. There were warm cherry scones with soft butter and Victoria plum jam, double chocolate chip muffins - warm and tasty, and lots more yummy treats.

I returned to my room and on my bed was a creamy gold ball gown with diamonds and rubies on it and around the neck and arms it had very elaborate frills. On the bed there was a diamond necklace that glittered like the stars in the sky on a pitch-black night. I got changed and when I came back out there was a woman standing there and she did my hair in curls. Then she put a beautiful silver tiara on me.

I looked out the window and there were two black limos with my name on them in diamonds.

Jade Barlow (12)
Birkenhead High School

A Day In The Life Of My Mum

It was an ordinary morning, just like any other, except I was in my mum's room. I got up and went to the mirror. I didn't feel myself and when I looked in the mirror you wouldn't even want to be in the same street.

I was in the body of my mum. I screamed so loudly I woke myself up and I saw myself in the doorway. I thought, *how can I be in two places at once?* I wasn't bothered about that, I was bothered about the fact that I had to live a day as my mum.

I had the day off but I still had to drop myself off at school. After that I went back home and tried to figure out a way to get into my own body again. I couldn't figure it out.

Just then the phone rang, I was scared out of my wits. It was work reminding me that I had a case tomorrow. Then I did some cleaning and, oh my God, it was half past three, I had to pick myself up. I whizzed down to school, going all over the road; well I had never driven before. I came back home scaring me and myself. When I stopped and thought for a moment I realised that *it really was hard being my mum!*

Zoe Howe (11)
Birkenhead High School

French Fake Wall Of China

China was outraged and forced to take action when the French started to build a rip-off 'Mur du Paris'; only a tenth of the real wall of China; they plan to build it around Paris.

Tourists' destination demands are differing nowadays. Resorts in China, Spain and America are on the rise, while the French tourism industry has dropped significantly. So not content with the only Disneyland in Europe, they are trying to gain more attractions. This is the thinking behind building a 'skit' of 'The Great Wall Of China'.

As from yesterday China's friendship with France was in jeopardy. China's daring midnight raid - stealing supplies from 'Mur du Paris' - has left the French traumatised and livid. They wonder why it is that China is so angry with them for building a 'wall'. The French have considered suing China for stealing their building materials.

China's reaction was, 'We will not give your construction material back until you stop your project of 'Mur du Paris.'

What do you suppose the French will do next if they are still not happy with all their 'fake' attractions? They might consider constructing a copy of 'Buckingham Palace'.

Rachel Kan (12)
Birkenhead High School

A Day In The Life Of . . .

It was horrific. Shops and cars, everything was destroyed. Lives washed away with the horrendous wave. All but ten houses that stood just outside of civilisation. They were odd houses. There was something slightly odd about the families who lived there too, especially young Amanda.

Amanda had curly ginger hair with freckles to match. She was very kind. The other children did not care though, and they called her names, this made her very upset. All she wanted was to be pretty and have friends. Having friends was now a distant memory for Amanda, her best friend had moved away.

Amanda woke up the day after the disaster had occurred. Then she realised that everything was certainly different, she was in a different room. This one was so much larger and grander than hers, the bed was no longer a small single but now a four-poster bed with violet drapes surrounding her.

She thought it must have been a dream so she pinched herself just to be sure. She felt a sudden pain in her arm; it couldn't be a dream, but where was she?

She climbed out of her bed and stumbled across the floor. It felt soft on her feet, she used to have wooden flooring but she was now walking on a cream carpet. When she looked in the mirror she didn't see herself but a woman with long brown hair, no more freckles, just golden brown skin, but who was she? She knew that she was rich by the size of the room and the objects inside, designer clothes, shoes and outfits. As she looked at herself she wondered, *who am I and who have I become?*

Gabriella Kitchen (12)
Birkenhead High School

A Day In The Life Of . . .

I was awoken suddenly by a noise coming from the bathroom. I stumbled in but there seemed to be nothing there. I glanced at my watch and it was nearly seven o'clock. Time to get up anyway, so I started to wash my face.

'Ouch!' I said, as my finger began dripping with blood.

I looked in the mirror and saw two big, sharp fangs. That explained what I had cut my finger on, but hold on, argh! Why have I got fangs? I must have turned into ... oh no, a lady version of Dracula.

I quickly walked into my bedroom so no one would see me in this state. Just then I suddenly had a strange feeling and my fangs started to tingle. Millions of things were rushing through my head ... thoughts of what a vampire could do.

I put my hand on my head with a force as the words sprang into my mind of what I wanted to do. 'I think ... I think ... I think I want to bite someone.' Suddenly I felt vicious as I started to hunt for somebody to sink my sharp teeth into.

An object caught my eye as I was walking past the window. It was a man, walking down the road. I grabbed his neck and bit him. 'Yuck!' I shouted, 'that tastes awful.'

I started to go dizzy. What was happening now? Then poof! I was me again.

I never want to be a Dracula again! I'd rather sink my teeth into a burger!

Ellie London-Smith (12)
Birkenhead High School

Mars Maths Maniacs!

A group of school teachers have been taking children to Mars to make them work as their slaves!

It has been found out today that a lot of pupils from Crossroads High School have been going missing.

It has been the teachers there, that are from Mars, that have been taking them there to work for them.

It has been a traumatic week for the pupils as some of the teachers have been kidnapping their best friends from the ordinary lessons that they are used to having.

Some of the pupils have been brought back, but not many, they would be very lucky if they were.

Some of the police have been in contact with the mathematics teachers but they still refuse to let the innocent victims go.

We interviewed one of the school children that had been present at several of the kidnappings and this is what he had to say, 'I was so scared of going into school the next day after the kidnapping. I tried to tell my mum but obviously she would not believe me. I had to go to school the next day terrified. I keep thinking that I will be their next victim!' exclaimed Daniel.

Gemma Madden (12)
Birkenhead High School

Help!

The thunder was growling. I was in the dark with my grandad. I was very scared. My grandad was showing me where he used to go to school; he told me that it was big and old.

As we got closer I could see it faintly. We got closer and nearer. It didn't look how my grandad had described it, as 'big', in fact, it looked enormous. I said to my grandad it looked haunted. He said it was all his school chums - he was just messing (I hope).

There were some men outside, next to the old stone wall. They said we could go in. So we did. When we went in through the big wooden doors my grandad showed me where he used to be taught maths. As we walked around I thought I saw a light behind me and I told my grandad but he said he couldn't see anything. We carried on walking. When we were walking past where my grumpy grandad used to be taught English, he told me about this boy that used to chase him into the caretaker's room.

I thought I saw the light again, only this time bigger. I told my grandad. This time he said that he could see it. We ran, the light was getting brighter and closer, rapidly. The light chased us into the caretaker's room. We turned around, then door locked behind us. There was an image of the boy. We were locked in.

Help!

Hannah McGuire (12)
Birkenhead High School

The Evil Unicorn-Opening Chapter

In a beautiful green wood there lived a snow-white unicorn. Wherever this unicorn travelled, kind, gentle and free-spirited animals followed.

This isn't a child's story. Alas, this is the true story …

In a dank, dark forest, where screams echo all around, lived a coal-black unicorn. The rabbits, deer and birds feared him, as did the many other unicorns. Thus, they all kept their distance.

Any creature could leave the vast forest. Any at all. All but one - the black unicorn, evil in heart, who would slay anything. He was a prisoner, an immortal prisoner. For centuries he had been imprisoned, and for many more that shall stand …

Until he learns to love and cherish a human, a certain human called John Robert Mores. However, no human has ever trodden on these eerie paths, many elders have seen to that.

As the curse that bestowed him says, 'Thou cursed unicorn, thou shalt stay in this now cursed forest. Thou shalt be doomed for all eternity. Thou shalt only be freed if and when thou love thy human. Thy human will stumble across thy path, and thy human will hunt for thy horn, thou shalt love the man I bestow upon thy wicked soul'.

He has waited, and waited, and waited. Wanting to be free, needing to be free. Waiting, and waiting, and waiting. A desire to be free, but a deep incapacity to love … an enigma, desperate to be solved …

Ruth Moots (12)
Birkenhead High School

A Day In The Life Of A Tsunami Victim

The majestic trees sway in the harmonious wind. Children dart along the beach, cascades of crystal blue water tumbling at their feet.

This is my life of beauty and tranquillity, my home, heart and family live here.

Padding across the golden sand, the sun beams its warmth and light. I see her! The Mary Sue, bobbing in the rhythmic sways of crystal blue water, her cracked paintwork glinting.

Jumping lightly into the boat, I push off from the damp sand. Silence echoes throughout. The whole world is holding its breath as the water suddenly starts to trickle away, ebbing backwards from the sea.

Moments later, my head in turmoil, the first fish flap, gasping for water on the drained seabed.

Turning around to peer into the distance, a spasm of uncontrollable terror grips my heart. Wrenching my head up towards the sky I pray for my family. I dash back to shore and all I can do is wonder. Is this the apocalypse? Has the hand of God finally struck, devastating the world?

A towering mass of water leaps up at my feet, this is no tidal wave, a fierce monster eccentric, reckless, inexplicable. My heart pounds, a solid wall of water is chasing me. The battered remains of the Mary Sue whip past me as the waves envelop my shattered body. My last glimpse is one of havoc as the wave strikes against the land. The beach crumples against its force, screams and more screams and then darkness.

Fenella Nance (12)
Birkenhead High School

Survivor

They looked into each other's eyes and his crying stopped. It was the first and last time they would see each other. The woman then passed her newborn baby son to seven-year-old daughter Etta, and closed her eyes.

Etta rummaged through the bins behind the restaurant, looking for something to eat. The hot African sun beat down on her back and made the rubbish smell.

'Get away from my restaurant, you animals,' shouted a waiter, pushing her away. Another night without food.

Etta was sixteen now and her brother nine, their mother had died before naming him. Etta called him Wanaoishi - survivor, because of his perseverance to stay alive.

'Tomorrow I'll get a job at the factory. We won't be hungry and maybe we can save up for a house,' said Etta. Wanaoishi smiled weakly, grateful for Etta's optimism.

'Wait here and do not move,' said Etta as she left Wanaoishi on his own, while she applied for the job.

Wanaoishi waited two days for Etta to come back, but she never did.

Wanaoishi searched for Etta for a year - living on the streets alone was tough. Local charity workers fed and clothes him and let him use the truck to look for Etta.

Then one day it happened. 'Stop!' screamed Wanaoishi. Was it really his sister?

He sprinted over, they embraced and wept in each other's arms - not sure if this was really happening.

Etta gazed into his eyes and said, 'My survivor.'

Lydia Parry (12)
Birkenhead High School

A Romantic Day In The Life Of Fido

I was just waking when I heard the small light footsteps I dreaded. It was Megan. I'm getting old now and as a Springer Spaniel, don't want to play as much. But Megan, well Megan always wants to play. Her favourite game is fetch, all she has to do is throw the stick but I have to run after it, find it and run back with it and repeat it all over again. My favourite is cuddling up to her and going to sleep.

She bounded up to me and gave me a cuddle and a stroke. After, she got my favourite breakfast, Doggyos, and sat down to watch TV. Soon after, Mum came down and made them both breakfast, which looked even worse today. Brown oaty things, yakk! Disgusting! Although sometimes food is quite tasty. I do occasionally like a bit of meat.

Lunch came and passed but then it was playtime. On went my lead and we went out into the freezing cold. We walked up the hill and over the other side until we came to the field. Megan soon found a stick and threw it as far as she could, which was quite far. As I ran I got slower and slower until I ground to a walk. It took me ages to find the stick and when I returned with it I was out of breath and panting. This time Mum threw it. I knew it would go further, it was like training for dog army, fetching again and again.

Finally they finished, but then the long walk back again I was dreading. On the way back a really funny thing happened, I walked past this dog and this amazing shiver went up my horizontal spine - she was beautiful, one of a kind. I had found it, true love! I daydreamed all the way home about her, her wonderful eyes and her sweaty dog smell.

All the rest was a blur, but all I know is that I can't wait to go out on a walk tomorrow!

Emma Robinson (12)
Birkenhead High School

Royal Retirement

For the last few weeks, the royal family have been told they are losing support from the people of England.

The Queen did as much as she could to get the respect of the people back. She lowered taxes and gave people who were earning less than £500 a month an extra £500.

None of this seemed to work. The Queen became tired and stressed. Recent pictures have shown the Queen being angry towards Charles.

The Queen and the royal family have been so tired that they did not have time for the royal corgis. They have been re-homed by Mr Jones in Birkenhead.

Last night the Queen revealed that the royal family were retiring.

Tony Blair is struggling to believe what he has just heard ...

'I am retiring as queen of England.'

Tonight at midnight the Queen will fly thousands of miles to Australia. She will stay there for the rest of her retirement. The whole royal family will accompany her on her trip and stay there also.

Tony Blair is doing his best to increase the taxes after the Queen ordered him to lower them.

Rioters are outside Number Ten, throwing eggs and other objects.

Blair told the press this morning that anyone with high importance should come forward to be king or queen of England. Please call 07986554564.

This day, 1st April 2005 will go down in history as one of England's worst nightmares!

Jocelyn Robinson (12)
Birkenhead High School

The Teachers From Ugg

On Monday 9th May, in Birkenhead High School, there had been some unusual sightings and noises taking place.

It was reported that teachers at Birkenhead High School were, in fact, impostors from the planet Ugg. Fellow students think that Mrs Lloyd (the English teacher) is one of them. The question is, why have they come here? What are their objectives? How did they get here? Do they have the same teaching abilities as the teachers on planet Earth?

Our scientists in the lab have been trying to work out why they are here. First indications are that they are a friendly type of alien who have come here to find out how the teachers at Birkenhead High School teach the children, so they can develop a similar type of education system back home on planet Ugg.

After two days of consideration, the scientists finally concluded that the teachers from planet Ugg do not pose a threat to the children of Birkenhead High School and only came here to planet Earth to improve their education system back on planet Ugg. Once this has been established, their visit to Birkenhead School Authority will provide a complete curriculum of teaching methods.

The teachers from Ugg contacted their planet and arranged for a spaceship to come and collect them. Prior to their departure, a party was arranged and a good time was had by all.

Hannah Rowlands (12)
Birkenhead High School

The Wave That Shook The World

They look straight into your eyes and although they cannot explain their heartache to you in English, their anguish is solemnly plain to see.

Please find my mother, my father, my brothers, my sisters ...

You learn to read their expressions, but what can you say to ease their fear that their loved ones will not be found?

After so many days since the tsunami struck, such consoling words would almost certainly be a lie. But still they plead with their dark, lonely eyes.

Walking through the streets of Phuket you suddenly realise the true extent of destruction that has been caused. Your senses numb and drift off into a trance. The desperate cries from families overwhelms you, the agonising images of children as young as three searching for food and water, grasp you tightly.

The tsunami struck on 26th December hitting the coast at speeds of 50mph. Hundreds of feet of sea floor was exposed, leaving sea creatures flailing desperately. Submerged rocks, reefs and even whole islands suddenly became visible as the killer wave hit the coast of Thailand!

Then came the disturbing pictures of beaches littered with bodies, mass burials everywhere you look to hinder the spread of disease and the lingering air of death surrounding you.

Now, looking over the wrecks of homes and villages you realise how lucky we are to have what we have. This truly was one of the most horrific natural disasters ... ever!

Georgia Smith (12)
Birkenhead High School

The Riddle Of The Forbidden Forest

(Opening chapter)

The sun rises over the horizon, bringing light to the Forbidden Forest on the hills of Doby village.

A treasure lies deep within the heart of the forest. A gate with a riddle on each side guards the entrance to the labyrinth leading to the Treasure of the Elements.

One man reached the labyrinth once but was doomed to roam in its walls, lost. He died not long after. Once you go in there's no way out unless you go back and answer the riddles on the other side of the gate.

A river runs by the gates and it has amazing powers to heal wounds. Some people have already drunk from its waters.

Fiona Dial, one of the young village girls, slipped away from Doby village one night and into the Forbidden Forest. She had always wanted to find out what wonders it held.

She came to the arch of the forest, which was the entrance and walked through the arch and into the mystic forest itself. The trail was damp and dark. Leaves lay on the floor covering her path, leading her straight to the gates. Animals called with strange eerie cries as one answered the other. The light had been drained away by the forest, making the path more and more treacherous ...

Jessica Yung (12)
Birkenhead High School

The American Coast - Toast!

It sounds like the plot of a Hollywood disaster film. A giant volcano erupts in the Canary Islands, sending a giant tsunami travelling faster than a jet aircraft across the Atlantic Ocean to the major population of the east coast of America, killing tens of millions of people and wiping out New York and Washington DC.

Except this is no film, it's reality. Scientists believe that the threat from the volcano of Cumbre Vieja on the island of La Palma is real and could send a huge slab of rock twice the size of the Isle of Man crashing into the Atlantic Ocean. Now what a disaster that would be! It would generate a huge wave with great energy. After travelling across 4,000 miles of the Atlantic for about nine hours, the great tsunami would hit the Caribbean Islands, the east coast of Canada and the USA with devastating effects.

It would stretch about 20 miles inland and destroy anything it its path.

The scientists were warning that the US government is not taking the threat from Cumbre Vieja seriously enough and not enough is being done to monitor it.

Professor Bill McGuire warned that Boston, New York, Washington DC and Miami could be virtually wiped out. He says close monitoring might at best provide two weeks of warning of the disaster but still despite knowing about it for a decade, no one has been keeping watch on the mountain.

Could this be the end for the American east coast?

Jemma Barnes (12)
Birkenhead High School

Manhattan Mystery

At 4am in Sarah Hihngity's house, Sarah sat bolt upright, her hazel hair falling forward onto her face. She groped around for her glasses, darkness looming in the apartment bedroom.

Sarah slid out from under the covers. She longed for Peter, the only one she had ever loved. However, he had died in a tragic rail accident exactly a year ago that day. She longed for his smile, his comforting words.

The usually bustling streets were deserted; the only sound was the rustling of the papers brushing against the sidewalk below. Sarah's throat burned as she turned to reach for a glass of water. She started to retch uncontrollably, she couldn't breathe, her chest was becoming tighter. The words *do not forget* rang in her ears. The breathless body of Sarah Higngity hit the floor with a thud ...

Edward Kourkinova, Sarah's brother and best friend left his apartment in Jinks Walk at 9.05 the following morning. He walked along New Regents Street to Manhattan City Centre; were Sarah lived. It was a long walk but Edward enjoyed the early morning stroll to college. He stopped outside Sarah's apartment as usual.

'Sarah, are you up there?' Edward climbed three flights of stairs to her flat. 'Sarah! Open up!'

Still no answer, so he pushed the door open. The sight that met him made him freeze. Suddenly his throat started to ache, his breathing became shallow and rapid. He couldn't breathe, scenes from his life flashing before him. The last moment of his life were a blur. He hit the carpet with a thud, his own blood trickling across his face ...

Laura Johnson (11)
Birkenhead High School

A Day In The Life Of Jesus

In the morning I awoke. The feeling of joy and happiness filled my body. My mother Mary made me breakfast of matzoth (unleavened bread) and water. I ate it quickly in order to have time to do my duties that God had given me.

The morning sound of birds chirping cheerfully filled the air and made me smile. I was going to meet Peter in the town centre to help him do some work.

I was walking slowly along the dusty dirt track when I saw a lady who was looking very ill and lying on the floor. I went over and asked her what the problem was. She was in severe pain. I prayed to God, I touched the lady on the arm and she was automatically healed.

I later made it to the town. Peter wasn't there, in fact nobody was there, something was going on! In the distance I saw a gathering of people. I made my way over to see what they were doing.

I saw some men, one was hanging off a large, crumbling, wooden tree. I said, 'What are you doing to that man?'

'Hanging him because he believes in God!' they replied.

In a rage I again spoke, 'Just because this man believes in God and not your god, doesn't mean that he is a bad man.'

'Yes it does, he should believe what we tell him to believe because he works for us!' they argued again.

I sorted the problem out! I later returned home and told my mother, Mary the whole story.

Kate Neave (12)
Birkenhead High School

A Day In The Life Of Abigail Dawson

This story is about a girl called Abigail Dawson. She was born in 1738 and is still living today. Instead of telling you about how she is now, let's go back in time to see how she lived then.

It was just an average day in the village of Waikiki, when screams of laughter came from the hilltops on the barren plains. This laughter was from the mouth of a man called Uric. He was a very simple man and enjoyed the country a great deal. So much in fact that he was sitting under a great oak at this very moment in time. The explanation for this laughing was Abi, the village pharmacist. She made the sick well; and was very well known throughout the lands of Tinchu.

Abi had run out of potions and had gone to Uric for the remedies to the illnesses that had spread throughout the village, as the crops had been taken away by the famine.

Uric was the only one to know about her secret, which was that she was a wiccain (witch). She could heal the sick so easily that populations went up by the hundreds.

Uric really was partial to her and enjoyed her company. He favoured her out of all the new young women and was convinced that he was going to marry her.

The next day, Uric decided to propose to Abi. She had to think about this but eventually said yes and they lived happily ever after.

Kelly Sayer-Hall (11)
Birkenhead High School

Black Survival

My whole body was burning. How could I have caught it? I did everything the doctor told me to do. I wore my mask, I stayed well away from all the fish and the dead, yet I still caught it. Every breath I took, I feared it would be my last. Every movement I made would send a raging fire up my body.

In the distance I could hear my mother's tears and the comforting voice of my father. She didn't deserve this. She had dedicated her whole life to the Bible, yet she had still lost two of her sons.

Oh how I missed Edward and William. The thought of them even then gave me courage to stand up to the plague and speak out, 'I am not afraid!' But now I could not even whisper, let alone shout. Every time I opened my mouth my jaw would seem to crack under the pressure of the movement.

Then I heard the slow, steady footsteps of my father's proud boots. Sometimes I even wondered if it was his boots which had saved him from this *Black Death.* I heard the door open and then the slow moan as the bed gave way under his weight. The growl of his voice reached my throbbing ears. 'You have to be strong my son, you have to live. Your mother would not be able to cope with yet another death.' There was a pause then he carried on, 'Your friend Mathew is in great trouble.'

As soon as those words reached my ears I knew I had to survive. All the might I had left seemed to burst from me. My ears could hear, my eyes could see, I could move everything I wanted.

My friend needed me. *Now!*

Rebekah Stott (12)
Birkenhead High School

A Day In The Life Of A Billionaire

It was 4 in the morning and I felt a rumble downstairs, it sounded like an earthquake. I went downstairs and it stopped. All of a sudden, I was dressed in pearls, diamonds and rubies. I had my ears pierced too and I looked rich!

Meanwhile my Uncle Luke was enjoying the luxuries of his king-sized bed, when he felt the rumble too, which was like an earthquake. he was dressed in jeans and plain white T-shirt; he looked like a normal person, not a billionaire!

It was morning and I woke to a wonderful view, in a luxury bed, looking at my Lamborghini and my Ferrari and my new 60ft yacht! As I walked onto my balcony, I saw a swimming pool as well. This was the life! I jumped in my pool and my phone stated to ring. Who would phone me? It could be Luke, should I tell him, keep on enjoying life as a billionaire or go back to my normal life?

I answered the phone and it was Luke. He told me that the strangest thing has happened to him and I told him exactly the same because I felt sorry for him since he had his wedding tomorrow! I told him to fly back to America, so we could swap back.

Just before I flew back to England I had one last swim and one last blast in my yacht and one last spin in my Ferrari. I got back home and I was thinking of my uncle and what a brilliant life he has.

Later that morning I woke up in exactly the same place and the time was exactly the same. That was strange!

Holly Williams (12)
Birkenhead High School

A Day In The Life Of A Koala

I lounged lazily on top of a lofty eucalyptus tree, chewing pensively on a leaf. I suddenly heard a babble of excited voices.

'Oh yes, I love the zoo!' said an excited voice.

'Koalath are my favourite animal,' lisped another, 'I love how they thwing from branch to branch like Tarzan!'

'Please, koalas don't swing from branch to branch,' drawled a smug, snooty voice, 'I know a great deal about them. They are endangered and not very intelligent.'

I sat up indignantly and craned my neck to see who was speaking. Through the bars of my enclosure I could see three humans grouped around my *Koala* sign. There was a girl with long black hair and a squashed up face which strongly resembled a pug. Also a younger girl with the same sort of hair, but a bright pink chubby face. I was also disgusted to see that the contents of her nose were dribbling over her top lip. There was also a skinny boy with horn-rimmed glasses and a bad haircut. Not intelligent? I'd show him.

I grabbed a vine and cautiously lowered myself down the creeper. When I had scrambled about half-way down I took a deep breath and flung myself into the air. My arms flung around wildly trying to grasp another vine. I plummeted towards the ground and collapsed in a heap.

'You see, I was right, a completely hopeless species,' the boy said in a voice of maddening superiority.

Note to self, I thought, *never do that again.*

Roisin Abbott (13)
Birkenhead High School

A Day In The Life Of An Adult

All Danielle ever wanted was to be popular in high school. Her best friend was a fat, bubbly boy named Kevin but Danielle longed to be friends with Courtney. Courtney was mean and blackmailed Danielle into doing her homework for her. Because Danielle worshipped her, she would always do it.

At home, Danielle found a rather peculiar sachet on her bed. She read the pack anxiously and read aloud, 'This wishing dust will make all of your dreams come true.'

That night, Danielle wished that she could be happy …

Danielle woke up the next morning and shouted, 'Mum, Dad?' but nobody seemed to reply. Her flat was small and cramped and looked as if a bomb had exploded. She then saw herself in the mirror and was shocked to see a beautiful, tall lady standing before her in her reflection. Suddenly, the phone started to ring …

'Did you have fun cleaning?' A familiar voice snarled sarcastically. 'You used to be my best friend, but then I didn't like you so I decided to trash your flat. By the way, it's your old pal Courtney.'

The girl that had been worshipped was the worst friend ever and had trashed her house that she didn't even know of. At that moment, a handsome young man swept Danielle off her feet.

'Who are you?'

'It's Kevin, your best friend and I will always love you.'

Danielle realised when she was fourteen years old again, that you don't have to be popular to be happy. Kevin and Danielle got married when they grew up and lived happily ever after.

Kim Chapman (13)
Birkenhead High School

Ariadne Jones's Diary

A fictional diary of Ariadne from the Greek legend of Theseus and the Minotaur. Her father, King Minos, demands a yearly sacrifice of Athenian youths and maidens to be fed to the Minotaur, a deadly beast which lives in a huge maze called the Labyrinth.

Daddy's Labyrinth-sacrifice time again. Wonder who will come? Daddy says the Athenians are getting too arrogant though, trying to get out. He says no one can escape from the Labyrinth.

Aha! Had an idea! Tie string to oneself and have somebody hold it outside! Of course, will not test this. Would be far too dangerous.

Met the sacrifices today. Women are all much too young and leggy, men mainly useless wimps. However, met Theseus - tall, dark and *incredibly* handsome. Thinks however, he can kill the Minotaur ... Ah! will tell Theseus today about yesterday's string-tying idea - see whether he wants to try it! After all it would be a shame to kill someone with such a nice tan and lovely muscles.

Theseus said yes! Tomorrow, will stand outside Labyrinth holding string for gorgeous Athenian warrior. He will do battle with the Minotaur! Then we will run away together!

Wonder which shoes I should wear? Would white or blue make me look more in the manner of Aphrodite? No. Ankles too fat for either. Full-length toga is the only option.

Wow! Have done it!

Also, amazingly, Theseus has not noticed how much of a mess my hair is! Wind on the boat has made it look a total disaster ...

Elizabeth Clark (13)
Birkenhead High School

A Day In The Life Of A Cat

Everyone was taking advantage of the bright, sunny morning, by embarking to the seaside. Many cats were excited; they were going on holiday with their owners.

'The big day today!' screamed my sister Miffy, jumping up and down like a kangaroo.

'I can't believe I'm marrying the cutest cat ever!' I exclaimed.

My friend Binka made my fur look irresistible! My mother's friend did my make-up.

'Snowy, we're leaving in a minute or two,' said my mum. I had just enough time to have some milk. Swiftly my owner Jeremy picked me up and put me in the car.

When we arrived, the car park was full. Fortunately Jeremy found a space. As I got out of the car I suddenly realised, 'My veil, it's not here!' I could feel my heart beating fast and furiously; I tried not to panic.

All Jeremy could hear was me, miaowing! Jeremy found it in the car, where I'd left it. Relief flooded through my tiny body.

I walked up the aisle linking arms with my father. Jeremy smiled at me gently; he knew this was the right thing to do.

There he was, Simon, my fiancé and now he was going to be my husband. The priest read out the marriage vows to Simon and me. This is definitely the best day of my life! We all ran outside to see a limousine waiting for us.

'Caribbean here we come!' shouted Simon.

Seven years later, Simon and I are still together!

Rebecca Gort (13)
Birkenhead High School

A Day In The Life Of ... My Dreams

Wisteria Lane was a typical rich American place and in June everyone was so excited to hear that Sophia Kennedy was buying the dead Mrs Hoober's house next door to Mr and Mrs Solise.

As the days went by, people were getting anxious and bored with waiting for her to arrive so Bree, Edi, Susan, Lynette and Gabrielle (whilst having their poker night) decided to organise a welcome party for Sophia.

All these women turned from complete desperate housewives to totally helpful women to get this party ready. They also got some help from their children but that was a disaster, so they just helped Edi, who refused to do any real work, because of her manicure.

Days passed after the arrangements were made and finally the big day had come, it was July 13th and Sophia would be moving to Wisteria Lane.

From nowhere a young girl appeared down the street joyously! Everyone realised it was me. I was Sophia! I looked around at the beautiful, large houses and the gorgeous plant-covered gardens.

Wisteria Lane was beautiful. I was so looking forward to living here. How could people say 13th was unlucky? It was the luckiest day of my life. In my dreams I've wished of coming to a lovely place like this, but then I realised it was still just a dream. It was an unlucky day I had been dreaming about a fantastic place; Wisteria Lane. I had lived a day in the life of my dreams!

Sophia Kennedy (13)
Birkenhead High School

Life On Saturn?

Over the centuries there has been superstition about life on other planets. Most would say it's a lie but there are others who think differently so to settle the matter, we sent two of our outer space enthusiasts to Saturn on the adventure of a lifetime. Their mission was to find life on Saturn.

The journey was shorter than was expected, with an immediate answer, so we met up with the travellers to find out about the trip!

'It was a real surprise being sent to Saturn and it took a lot of adapting too but the results were amazing,' commented Mr Roach, one of our chosen explorers.

'The food was a total disaster and we were total novices to life away from Earth,' Mr Sloth agreed, 'however we learnt from our mistakes!'

'We experienced several meteorites passing us by, but generally the atmosphere was calm but full of excitement! However, the landing did frighten us, with lights flashing and alarms roaring, we thought we could be stranded on Saturn, living off compressed food but that idea changed completely.'

'Yes,' Mr Sloth continued, 'as soon as the first alarm was sounded, about ten aliens lifted the rocket into some sort of repair ship and it was as good as new! The aliens were really welcoming to us and even gave us accommodation at a three hundred and three storey high hotel with dinner included.'

'The technology was incredibly impressive, everything used electricity, luckily they had never had a power cut!' Mr Roach finished.

So our superstitions were finally revealed to be true! There really is life on other planets. What an amazing breakthrough!

Megan Morrison (12)
Birkenhead High School

A Day In The Life Of A RNLI Boat

As the huge orange boat slapped the waves, I could see a half sunken yacht with the man on top of the mast swinging around like a chimpanzee. We drove our motorboat onto the yacht's deck as the RNLI member went up after him ...

The pressure was too much. The yacht's mast fell onto the RNLI boat. The boat tipped under the water with the RNLI boat following after. After roughly 10 seconds the RNLI boat popped up. One of our men was under water fighting for the sailor's life, then the RNLI man popped up with the sailor unconscious. We wheeled him up with care.

After arriving back from the horrific incident 2-3 hours later, they got another call reporting 2 speedboats has collided, then one had burst into flames. All the crew went to the other speed boat.

The team on the RNLI boat jumped onto the speed boat. The tide was out. The boat's wheels drove on the sand to sea. The boat crashed the waves. The boat tipped side to side like a roller coaster. Then we saw it, a boat on fire. There were about 10 people standing with their life jackets on waving at us. They screamed and shouted. As we got closer I could hear them shouting, 'She's under water!'

We raced there and a crew member went under water as we grabbed the crew, the waves overlapping the boat, making it harder. The moist, cold air sent a chill down my spine as the woman was brought up ... *dead.*

Jessica Ollerhead (13)
Birkenhead High School

Short Story

'Make sure you have more money on you then, fat boy!' Brian yelled and swung his fist into my stomach. I doubled over and my eyes watered.

'Ha! Fatty's crying,' yelled Adam and Simon laughed over-enthusiastically.

Determinedly, I stood up straight and watched them walking down the road, pushing each other into the road and laughing. Grabbing my chance, I turned around and sprinted home as fast as I could manage, hoping that I wasn't too late.

As soon as I got to the door, it flew open.

'There you are! I thought you might have gotten lost. School is a long walk from here you know.'

'Hi, Mum!' I smiled, hoping I didn't look as hot as I felt. I glanced at her as I stepped into the house. She looked tired and her hair was at odd angles, like she had spent the day running her fingers through it. She saw me watching her and flashed me a smile that didn't make it to her eyes. 'So how was your day then?'

How could I tell her the truth?

'It was great! I got an A* in my French project, because Simon helped me. We had PE today too. I played football today and I scored the winning goal. Brian, Adam, Simon and I bought ice creams after school to celebrate.'

My mum smiled - a proper one that took away the anxiety in her face. 'Good, I'm glad. I'm proud of you, Tom.'

Naomi Phillips-Howard (13)
Birkenhead High School

Untitled

(Re-written chapter from 'PS I Love You' by Cecilia Ahern)

It has been one month Holly thought as she lay alone in the warm double bed. One month ago she was with Gerry, his warm hands and soft skin against hers, as he lay in the hospital bed, closer to death each second.

Gerry had been complaining of a headache for over a week when Holly told him to visit a doctor. The news was awful. The cause for Gerry's constant headache was a brain tumour.

Although Gerry was now gone, Holly knew they would always be soulmates. Silence was deafening. All she could hear were the occasional creaks of the floorboards and the sound of envelopes being forced through the letterbox by the impatient postman. She lazily dragged herself out of her cosy bed and onto the chilly wooden floor.

Blinded by the sun shining through the thick double-glazed window, Holly made her way downstairs to open the mail. *Another lonely, depressing day,* she thought to herself as she picked up a bunch of bills, sympathy cards and advertisements.

As Holly sat down at the kitchen table, she noticed a small white envelope standing upright against a glass vase of pink lilies. It read: *Even though I am gone, I will always be watching over you. PS, I love you.*

Gerry is right, she thought, *although he is gone he will always be with me because everyone needs a guardian angel.*

Solmaz Sajjad (13)
Birkenhead High School

A Day In The Life Of My School Bag!

After a nice restful night, I awoke from the sound of the alarm clock. I heard Ellie scramble out of bed. She walked over to the door and opened it sluggishly. I yawned and stretched out my handles. I felt down, it was a Tuesday, there were so many single lessons and all those books. I don't think I could cope with another one! It was as if the weekend was miles away. I knew that I would be the one that had to do the most work in the family! Why did Ellie pick me up? I could have been a travel bag, sailing the seas!

Ellie returned, dressed and ready to face Tuesday, it's just a shame I wasn't. She loaded the heavy books into me and flung me over her shoulder. I was heaved into the boot of the car and driven to school. I suppose it's better than walking.

When we arrived at school, I was thrown onto the table and I thought how ungrateful humans are. It was time for our first lesson history, second geography and so on!

It was ten-past one, lunchtime. After a long day of being dragged from classroom to classroom and teacher to teacher, it was home time! Great! Mum was waiting in the car park and I was left slumped in the boot. Only three more days till the weekend! It is OK after all I suppose, being a school bag!

Ellie Jacques (12)
Birkenhead High School

A Day In The Life Of A Puppy!

My new owner opened the front door and stood there was my worst enemy ... the postman. I ran out after him, but he had disappeared before I had reached the lawn.

After I had eaten that slimy, disgusting stuff they call food, I was allowed to go out in the garden. It was strange, my owner actually came out and swamped me with toys. Just as I was starting to get suspicious, I was locked up in a cold metal cage and whisked into the car. We arrived at a building with a large sign outside which reach *'Vet'*. My memory tracked to the last time I came here. Then I remembered clearly that this was where they shot long pieces of metal into me.

Just as I was being carried through the door, a cat sneered sarcastically at me, 'Good luck with the vaccinations, wimp.'

I was placed on a cold, uncomfortable table. I yelped and barked with nerves. A man dressed in a white overall slid the metal rod into my leg. This must be what they call vaccinations. Just as I was getting over the shock, another needle was inserted into me. Then I was allowed to go home and relax for the day, even though I needed a week to recover from the shock.

When bedtime came round, I snuggled up in my basket and dozed off to sleep thinking about today's trauma, hoping tomorrow would be better. Oh, it's a tough life for a puppy.

Emily Dixon (13)
Birkenhead High School

Miss America

The large droplets of rain drummed on Alice's window. It was November 1967 and at last, Alice was finally a teenager, yet she had no presents and no friends over that day. She just knew that her mother had forgotten her birthday altogether. Last month it had been her mother's birthday; Alice had remembered that! She had spent ages trying to find exactly the right words in the card and then chosen the present with real care. She had bought a box of Cadbury's chocolates, and a card that sang 'Happy Birthday' in a very high-pitched voice. They had gone to the new restaurant, 'The Leaning Tower', which was lovely; it actually leant to one side, and inside they served the most luxurious, mouth-watering pizzas you have ever tasted. Alice's mum and dad had just split up and since *that* day, nothing had been the same ...

Alice lived in a minute flat in London. Her mum was called Joan.

'Why do you make things so difficult for me, Alice?' questioned Alice's mum.

Of course, it wasn't Alice at all. Lately her mum and dad had been having fights all the time. Her dad would come in, often in the blackest of moods, and be very violent with Joan. He had threatened to kill them both if he ever saw either of them again ...

'Alice, stop daydreaming,' shouted Alice's mum.

Alice's arm was red from the smack her mum gave her. It was throbbing with pain. She followed her mum out of the old flat and down the old, rickety, wooden stairs (which she was sure were on the verge of breaking). They finally reached the bottom into the reception area, moving slowly towards the heavy, ornately grafittied door. Her mum forced the grubby wet door open. Into the silent, dismal room came the noise of a loud bustling street with plenty of tourists, all with thick brown raincoats on, fighting against the wind and hurling themselves into the shopping store where they were warm and dry. Alice turned to see her mother striding down the steps into the wind and rain; she quickly followed. After just a few minutes, they were drenched through by the incessant rain. Alice looked like a drowned rat by the time they had reached the other side of the road. It was a dismally damp journey, and when they finally reached the supermarket, Alice looked like she had been swimming in a lake, in her clothes!

Malika Ben Kahla (12)
Deyes High School

The Magic Feather

'Grandad!' shouted Lily and James. 'Tell us another story, please.'

'OK, OK,' said their grandad, 'calm down. Right, here we go, Goldilocks and the Three Bears. There were once three bears ...'

Ding! Dong! went the bell.

'Mail!'

Their grandad collected the mail from the local postman and then walked back into their bedroom. The way he looked at the letter he was reading told Lily and James there wouldn't be another story.

'Shall we go to sleep, Grandad?' asked James.

Their grandad replied, 'Yes, I've got a lot to think about. Goodnight.'

In the morning, Lily and James woke to find their grandad rummaging through their trunks and packing two suitcases.

'Are we going on holiday, Grandad?' asked Lily.

'I'm sorry, but I'm sending you on an extraordinary adventure. Your father and I have both done the same as you are about to do. I know you don't understand, I mean you're too young to understand, but out there, out there in another part of the world is a small feather full of all your hopes and dreams. You have to collect it before the next full moon, or it will be lost forever. With the letter was a map and a list of things you'll need. It also mentioned that someone else is after the very same thing, and it's up to you two to get to it first.'

'Grandad, I'm scared, I don't understand. What do we do? Where do we go? Who are we going with?' panicked James.

'Look, I've been given very little detail, all I know is that you're wasting time! Go on, go to the docks. There you will meet my best friend, Captain Liam. He will tell you the rest. Now, hurry on, go forth and make me proud.'

Laura Lovelady (12)
Deyes High School

The Loch Ness Monster

Once upon a time there was a monster. He was a friendly monster who would never castigate anyone. One Saturday afternoon he went on holiday, not just a holiday like you and me go on, a holiday to remember, and so he went to Scotland.

The next night, he went for a swim in Loch Ness; he was having a really pleasant time. He then felt famished for food. Five minutes later, he came back with a delectable delight. This was a delicious fish, and he started to eat it with joy. After another swim, he began to feel very tired and went to sleep.

The next morning, just as he was about to go home, he realised he was bigger than he had ever imagined; he had filled the whole three mile lake that he was in, he panicked and panicked, but in the end he had to stay in Loch Ness.

1,500 years later, he is still there. His nickname is Nessie. People go and visit him when they are on a pleasant holiday in Scotland.

Phillippa Jarvis (12)
Deyes High School

The Forest

The children ventured deeper into the forest as the wind howled and a cold breeze swept through it. Lucy got a cold shiver down her spine as if a freezing finger had drawn an etched line down her back. She didn't feel right. 'Maybe we should go back, I have a strange feeling about this. I feel a bit nauseated anyway.'

Suddenly, Anna had tripped and fallen, her eyes widened as a frantic sound of scuttling approached her. She was caught up in the twisted and gnarled fingers of the towering trees. She spoke quietly and softly, reassuring herself she would be OK, but deep inside, her gut-feeling was saying different, as she felt trapped and caged in the arms of the forest. The scuttling was now gaining speed and echoing around her. The floor started cracking, like it was splitting in half, its open jaw waiting for her to feed it, bellowing and beckoning her in.

Lucy clenched her fist as she watched her friend slowly disappear into the darkness. A tear trickled down her cheek, she felt so helpless and just wanted to save her, but she was so petrified her body wouldn't allow her to do anything. She was so speechless, she couldn't move her mouth. It felt as if her frozen jaw had locked itself closed.

Anna, now screaming in desperation, stretching her arms out as the malevolent hole buried more of her, had only to look in Lucy's eyes to see there was no way she could help her. At that moment, Ann had never felt so alone or guilty. She mumbled to herself strange things, as if in a foreign language, but Lucy still was able to make out of the complicated sentences, 'this is solely my fault'. As their tearful eyes met for the last time, they both became tenacious and determined to find each other one day.

Tyra Stevens (12)
Deyes High School

A Day In The Life Of My Pet

Bang! My dad had fallen out of bed again, so I gave him a bark to shut him up. It took him a whole five minutes until he managed to come downstairs and let me out into the garden.

In the garden, I beat my mate Patch five times in wrestling, and two times in a race, then my dad called me in halfway through a race. He shouted at me for being late, but we forgave him and gave him a walk and checked the wee-mail. I told that Labrador, again, to stay off my hedge, or else I'll have to sort him out! I left a message for my mate next door because he was out when I got back. My master came down, so I gave him a big lick to let him know I was still hungry, and eventually Mum gave me my breakfast.

When they left, they didn't shut the door tight, so my mate Patch, who can be clever at times, opened the door and we went upstairs. We laid on the big bed in the sunshine most of the time. I enjoyed saying hello to every dog that went past, without being told to be quiet. We also made a big mess on the bed with all the rubbish in the wastepaper bin. *Hee, hee, hee!* But I got shouted at when they got home. We were then put into the garden again and Patch found the best smell in the garden, and I chased those birds out of my garden again, but Dad gave them more food.

When we were called in, we had another wrestling match inside, but we got told off for playing in the house. Then my master came home, so I said hello to him to let him know I was here, and I watched TV with my master while waiting for tea. I always wait under the table in case my master slips me some food when he is eating, and then I challenged Patch to whoever could eat their food first. Patch always wins, but he has to burp! - No manners!

They put us out again to go to the toilet. They seem to think we need the toilet all the time, even in the rain. My mate Patch doesn't like the rain.

Then back to the TV. I particularly like the programmes with animals in them; my favourite is Crufts.

After supper, we are up till 11 o'clock, before we start to get too sleepy and go to bed on the settee.

Peter Hill (12)
Deyes High School

Beauty Contest With A Fight!

The beauty contest in Deyes High School, Maghull, was won yesterday by a young girl in Year 7, Hannah Flanagan (my best friend). She was overjoyed when she heard her name being called out.

My other friend, Ashley O'Neill, came in tenth place and was very annoyed. She stormed onto the stage and dragged poor Hannah's crown from her head, scratched all of her face then said, 'Look at the winner now, that ugly thing. I should have won!'

Hannah replied, 'No Ashley, this is a beauty contest, not an ugly contest!'

Hannah snatched her crown back off her and walked off the stage, leaving Ashley stood there with the whole school and the BBC watching her! I followed Hannah off the stage and got a few words from her.

'Did it surprise you when Ashley robbed your crown and scratched your face?'

'Yes, it surprised me, but I guess she was just jealous of my good looks.'

'I thought you two were good mates?'

'Yes we were, but I'm not sure about that now!'

Well, a beauty contest with a fight happened here yesterday, I don't think they will want another contest next year!

Danielle Evans (12)
Deyes High School

The Headless Horseman

It's night-time, the cold icy wind slices through the air like daggers puncturing flesh. The trees are bending and howling at the pain of their age. The old, spine-chilling colours of death painted on the walls. Dead bodies lying in the chambers, innocent people's heads cut off and stuck onto a spear. The Carnivorous Carnival of Sleepy Hollow is dying, it hasn't been given a human being to feast upon in a long time. No more victims who are going to be put into unbearable pain. But this is all going to change. Very, very soon ...

It's three o'clock in the morning, Zack is awake. He can't get to sleep; he reaches to his remote to see what's on television. He presses the 'power' button. Big mistake ...

The next day, Zack comes downstairs for his breakfast, his eyes wide open, not blinking, not breathing, not human. He misses breakfast. he walks straight out of the door, not knowing why. In his mind are just the words, 'Go to carnival ... go to carnival ... on the ghost train ... surprise.' He walks down his house path, not knowing that he's walking himself to his own death. The weather is snowy; thin white snow which seems like it will never stop falling, it is as white as a smouldering star in space. He strolls down roads unknown even to him. He gets to the gates of the carnival, he rolls his hand through the bars as he walks past. He is totally oblivious to a spear which has found its way through a single human head, upright as one of the fence poles, and there is no body to be seen anywhere. He can just see through the fence, a white mist and black towering trees bending over the fence, like it's being drawn into some kind of magic curse.

Zack walks into the carnival like a robot and looks for the ghost train. He spots it; it's behind this old, rusty gate with heads on spikes all around it. Enough to keep anyone away, but Zack, he has a mission. He walks through the haunted pathway, only to see a man on a horse, dressed in black. With no head. With one clean swipe, he slices through the boy's head with his sword, as easy as a knife cutting cheese. The headless horseman stabs his sword through the head and darts off into the mist, leaving the body to rot into the soil ...

Now that was a surprise Zack wasn't expecting ...

Andrew Evans (12)
Deyes High School

Brainstorming

16.40

I really can't think of what to write! I've been through everything: A Day in the Life of ... Myths and Legends (well I didn't, but I don't like them anyway!), A Newspaper Story, and there's only short stories left. I mean, what's a short story? Is it like, 'We went to the park and we fell over ...'? Because that's a short, and it's a story!

16.44

Still not thought of an idea! The wind's picking up now and it's sending the trees into next week! They're dancing and swaying, jumping! Aww, some poor bird's just been caught in the gale and been blown backwards! There are clouds gathering now, big, frowning black ones, all sticking to each other like pins to a magnet. They swirl and gather, as if to try and keep each other warm.

16.51

A thick stream of lightning just parted the sky! Thunder booms, breaking the uneasy silence in the air. A bird crows, but is cut short by numerous strikes and crashes. The sky is the darkest of the darkest. Now the heavens have opened, down falls sheet after sheet of rain. Thunder rumbles, forks of lightning are shooting across the sky, making the blackness not so black.

17.02

A high-pitched, blood-curdling scream comes from nowhere as another fork of lightning reaches out. A loud, final boom, crack and a crash. The storm is over, but the moment isn't. Some loud, painful sobs come from down in the garden. Oh no! That is when I realise I don't have a chimney anymore ...

Fiona Wileman (12)
Deyes High School

Grand Parents

It was a crisp November morning when, after a seven hour trans-Atlantic flight, Louise arrived in frosty England.

The London sights did nothing to lift her spirits; the prospect of staying with her great aunt and uncle filled her with dread. Her mom and step-dad were on vacation in sunny Cyprus, and in their wisdom, decided to arrange the visit despite Louise's protests. After the last visit, she swore she would never return. Aunt Beatrice and Uncle George were in their eighties; they did not understand the fun a thirteen-year-old girl craved. Last time, when she was finally allowed to leave her room, she had to endure mind-numbing trips to the museum. Louise thought Beatrice and George should be in a museum.

Wearily she made her way up the steps to the front door. It seemed like an eternity waiting for her aunt and uncle to answer the door, as they were far from sprightly.

As Louise stepped into the hall, the smell of polish and lavender filled her nostrils. She followed her uncle, who shuffled like a zombie from the movie she saw on the plane. At the foot of the stairs she was greeted with an embrace from her silver-haired, deaf aunt.

'Why don't you go upstairs and unpack dear. I'll bring you up a cup of lemon tea,' she croaked.

Yuck, Louise thought, she would rather have a can of Coke.

Louise made her way up to her bedroom. It was an old but simple room with a wooden bed and set of drawers, almost the same as last time, however the old drape curtains had disappeared and in their place was an old crooked door. it was a dark shade of brown with a hefty brass handle, and right in the centre was a distinct letter 'B'. Louise rubbed her hand across the ancient door and amazingly, it opened. The room was dark and had an eerie feeling about it. She could just make out a tiny lustrous light in the far distance. She started walking towards this mesmerising light. She could feel a cold, trickling shiver down her spine; she knew she shouldn't be there, but it was too late to turn back. She kept walking until she ended up in a forest.

Soon her eyes adjusted to the light. She looked around; there was nothing, except thick pine trees. But then in the corner of her eye, she saw a shivering, enigmatic silhouette. It was coming towards her. She ran for dear life, when suddenly ...

Sarah Welsh (11)
Deyes High School

The Malevolent Hunter Of Midnight

Dodging razor-sharp willow branches, we entered the forest of death. Too many lives had been pinched by the malevolent hunter of midnight. I'm usually verbose, but tonight was different! Many brave knights had tried to rid us of the inhuman killer, but not one had prevailed.

The howling of the wind grew louder and the atmosphere turned colder, like someone or something was watching us from the dense undergrowth.

We knew it was forbidden to enter this eerie, never-ending forest, let alone be out at night. Silence. The hairs on the back of my neck stood on end. A hand, a slimy, hairy, nail-bitten hand lay trembling on my thin, bony shoulder. I froze. Every horror film I had seen darted through my head. And then it happened ...

I suddenly let out a humongous scream. Run, run, run! All I could think of was to be ensconced. It means to hide in safety. Miss Batt hammered it into us at school. School. If only I was in the ancient, rotten gates of Little Apple School. But I wasn't! I ran as fast as my stick-like legs could carry me. Closer, closer. Whatever it was, was gaining on me. I was like a hunted fox; all I could do was run!

Why did I let my brother force me into the hunter's forest anyway? Why couldn't I have stood up to him for once? 'David, David, *help!*'

My voice echoed through the fingers of the trees, but there was no reply.

Hazel Miller (12)
Deyes High School

The Enigmatic Loch Ness Monster

I was on my holidays, up, in and around Scotland, visiting three different places: Fort William, Fort Augustus and Lossiemouth. I was going with my dad and his friend Sowers. We were visiting Fort William to climb Ben Nevis, Fort Augustus to view Loch Ness, and Lossiemouth to visit relatives.

When we turned up at Fort Bill, we immediately set up camp and paid for our stay at the foot of Ben Nevis.

The next day, Saturday, we rose early, about 5am, and headed off to the summit. The walk was tiring and all three of us were feeling rather lethargic, so we went into the nearest pub and ate our meal.

On Sunday, we had to pack away our tents and head off to Fort Augustus. We were still feeling sluggish from our long walk the day before.

Whilst we were approaching Fort Augustus, we stopped at a deserted sight-seeing point, changed drivers and ate lunch. I was now taking a great interest in the water, when I saw a great big, iniquitous-looking, enigmatic, glutinous, snaky thing emerge from the cold water. I screamed, *'Look!'*

'Sweet Jesus of Nazareth,' they simultaneously replied.

'Right, we're going straight to Lossie,' said Sowers in an alarmed way, wheel-spinning away.

'Great idea!'

Ben Bowker (12)
Deyes High School

Pegasus And The Triclops

One day, a Greek man called Pegasus, was walking through his town square when he saw his town's most beloved valuables being sold on a stall. He asked the man why they were being sold.

'The town is so short of money lately that we have to sell these items to collect more money for food.'

Pegasus thought this was terrible, so he decided to make his own stall; a stall for weapons, because his speciality was making weapons and this was handy because he was such a fine warrior. The first thing he decided to make was a bow and arrow. As he was loading the bow, his hand slipped and the arrow shot straight across the market and hit Prince Nazeem in the centre of his chest. Everybody ran to the prince and he was rushed to the village hospital.

Pegasus could not sleep that night for guilt and in the morning it got worse, he received news that the prince had died late last night. When the rest of the town found out, they were furious and everybody hated Pegasus from then on.

One year later, Pegasus had gone into hiding and he lived in a small hut on the edge of the village.

The town crier was screaming the next day that a triclops had been sighted on the edge of town. Pegasus thought quickly, *If I can kill this monster, then everyone in the town will like me again.* He spent the remaining hours making weapons of all different kinds.

Within hours he was back, stumbling into the town with the three-eyed monster's head in his arms. The whole town cried with happiness and Pegasus was forgiven, and things were back to normal again until the day he died.

Joel Taylor (12)
Deyes High School

Everton - 4th Place Is Ours

Moyes' men secure 4th place after Liverpool got beaten 3-1 by Arsenal. However, Everton never really did any better when they faced the Gunners. A 7 goal thriller as Everton got humiliated by Arsenal 7-0 at Highbury. David Moyes told us, 'After our 2-0 win over Newcastle, I felt I needed to rest the likes of Martyn and Cahill for the tournament in Thailand'.

Manchester City are also heading to Thailand for the tournament, after Robbie Fowler's stoppage time missed penalty that sent their UEFA cup dreams crashing down, in their 1-1 draw against Middlesbrough at the City of Manchester Stadium on Sunday.

Another loss for Mr Moyes, as Everton got back 3-2 at Bolton's Reebok Stadium. Everton are the first ever team to go into the Champions League with a negative goal difference of -4. What will the tournament have in store? We will have to wait and see.

Thomas Williams (11)
Fazakerley High School

Drive-By Car Crash

Last night at 11.30pm, local man Andrew Jones was killed in a drive-by after leaving the bar drunk. Witnesses describe the car as a black Audi TT, with spoiler, small exhaust pipe, silver rims and a built-in blade on the door handle, which can only be opened by a switch on the bonnet.

Mr Jones' colleague says that Mr Jones has been part of a gang and drug business and that could be why he was killed.

After the drive-by, the car took a skid and hit another car and simply just drove off, causing many other cars to spin out of control and crash. The victims were left until an ambulance arrived. Fortunately the passengers were OK, but the driver was seriously injured. Andrew Jones had a family, a wife and two children. He worked in a nightclub and was 28 years of age.

The police are still searching for the gangsters, but haven't yet had any luck. A report by another witness was that the gangsters were last seen on Bakon Road. Police are willing to hire anyone willing to go undercover and find out what the gang are going to do, so the police can track down and capture them. The police are desperate to catch the gang, since this is not the first violent crime they have made to murder someone. They have destroyed the community.

If anyone suspects someone doing anything, come to the police station on Skint Street, or contact Crimestoppers.

Vincent Giang (12)
Fazakerley High School

My Life As A Dolphin

Years passed as I was born, growing up and admiring where I lived. I was very excited, probably due to the fact that I knew lots of other dolphins in my family. There was my mum, dad and lots of other friendly dolphins, but one day in this extraordinary life of mine, my two best friends were lost.

When I found out what had happened to them, I was miserable and didn't talk to any of my family or friends, because I had spent my whole life with my living parents. Now they were gone forever - never to be seen again.

I decided that when I had my children, they would stay by me, because I didn't want them to get caught in a fishing net and be ... killed, like my mum and dad. This made me sure that I would always protect and love my babies because if anything ever happened to them, I would ... I don't know what I would do, or how I would survive.

It had all basically started when fishers had come to collect their monthly load of fish. My mother and father were admiring the coral reef, when all of a sudden the nets caught them and ... well, they were killed that day.

This is why I am giving a message out to all you humans to never harm or kill your family or friends. Just protect and love them.

Lana Dewsbury (12)
Fazakerley High School

The Red-Armoured Knight

Once there was a knight and he was the most feared knight in Dundersville. Many knights had challenged him, none had won the challenge. He (we all thought it was a he because of his talent) had lately been challenged by a woman called Jacqueline. The red-armoured knight decided to go easy on her. He got out his sword and shield, then climbed on his horse. He galloped into the stadium and took a leap off his horse.

'Let the fight begin,' said the leader. 'Remember, people, there are no rules here.'

The fight began. The knight was unaware of this, but Jacqueline had started before the bell. The knight was prepared for this. Jacqueline pulled out an extra sword and went to stab the knight, but the knight held up his shield and smashed it down onto Jacqueline and her sword. The sword smashed into pieces.

'Jacqueline will be penalised for using a fake sword,' shouted the leader.

'There are no rules,' complained Jacqueline.

'They just made some, sorry, but I'm allowed to have another weapon.' The knight chose a lion.

He sent the lion at the woman and the lion swallowed her without chewing once. Since the challenger had been swallowed whole, the knight had to defeat the lion. But then the lion was cut in half and Jacqueline jumped out. She stabbed the knight will all her strength.

'Argh!' the red knight shouted in pain. The knight stabbed Jacqueline and that was the end.

Mark Thomas (12)
Fazakerley High School

King Arthur's Disasters

There once was a king called Arthur. He was in love with the Princess Joy. One day after a shocking thunder storm, King Arthur asked, 'What do you want today, my sweet?'

Joy replied, 'I would love a branch from the singing oak tree.'

So off Arthur went to get the branch.

He was on his journey for about seven days and eight nights until at last he found the singing oak tree. But little did Arthur know that there was a pack of black bears nearby, and all Arthur whispered was, 'Shut up, I'm planning how to get one of those branches for Princess Joy.'

While he was looking for the perfect branch, he saw Robin Hood and his merry men. They were having a party, killing the most ugly dragon they had ever seen. While they were enjoying themselves, Arthur sneaked over to the nearest branch, pulled out his sword and started to chop off the branch. Suddenly, Little John saw the king cutting off one of the branches, so he sounded the alarm. Everyone rushed to Little John and said, 'What's the matter?'

'Someone has cut off the Tom Jones' singing branch,' he answered.

When King Arthur returned, he gave Joy the branch a he asked, 'Joy, will you marry me?'

Joy replied, 'Maybe.'

'Yes, I'll start the plans,' Arthur shouted. 'Hold the phone, did you say yes, no or maybe?'

'I said maybe,' she said.

'OK, I'll see you later, Buttercup.'

Gary Gibbons (12)
Fazakerley High School

A Day In the Life Of A Royal Marine

It was a beautiful day on HMS Red Dragon. It was Friday 13th, an unlucky day for some. It was hard to believe we were at war, but we were, so we were going to have to get used to it. Seeing as it was Friday 13th, everything was going wrong. We had an inspection and today I was really dreading it. Why today of all days? It would have to be today!

The inspector first went to my friend's bunk, it went really well for him and he received a promotion, but as for me, I received a promotion the following day.

I really had to do the best I could, otherwise I would have to go back to my normal post. I was cleaning my area over and over again. There was only one little corner that let it down. The inspector walked up to me and my area, he looked around and then walked away.

The admiral shouted, 'Drill time!' We ran outside onto the deck and lined up. He shouted, 'Five hundred press-ups, now!' Only then it happened, the torpedo hit.

'Red alert! Red alert!' It was going off everywhere.

The captain ran to the front of the ship and shouted, 'The ship is sinking!'

We jumped into the lifeboats and tried to row away, but it was too hard. The ship was sucking us down with it. We were pulled deep under the water.

I was the lucky one as I was the only survivor.

Alex Baines (12)
Fazakerley High School

The Second World War

In the Second World War, many kids had been taken to different places because the Germans had been bombing us. The Germans had bombed the navy, so they could not have food. Some kids and babies had died because of the shock and terror.

Most of the time, people had to wear gas masks because the smoke could have killed them. Lots of ships had been bombed, which led to people being drowned on the ships because they could not get out. People used to wait forever to come out of the bomb shelters.

Then one day there was a miracle, because we had won the war and we had a big party in the streets. It was called VE Day, which means victory in Europe.

Beth Dawes (12)
Fazakerley High School

On The Run

One day, my mum, my little brother and I were walking to the shop on the way home from school. We got the usual lolly ice for Timmy, and a Magnum for me, and a scratch card for Mum. While we were in the shop, Mum scratched the card off and she won. Her eyes glowed.

'What is it, Mum?' I said.

'I've won £110,000!'

The shopkeeper said, 'What? Let me see ... yes, you have.'

Mum said, 'Come on, we are going shopping.'

Then I said, 'Are we going to tell Dad?'

'No, we are not!' she shouted. 'We are going to run away and we will get different identities.'

We went shopping, then Mum said, 'We will get the 9pm train to London.'

We went for something to eat, then got to London at about 1am.

In the morning, we got different identities. We stayed in London and I have never seen my dad since. The reason we left was because Dad was hitting Mum.

Alex Bilsborrow (11)
Fazakerley High School

It's All Over For iPod!

Nokia, the giant phone company have said they are to bring out a new model, the Nokia N91 Jukebox.

The N91 Jukebox obviously has a jukebox. The jukebox allows singles and albums to be downloaded wirelessly from the internet.

The Apple iPod has already sold nearly four point two million models worldwide. It could either have a 2gb memory, or a 20gb memory. Many people however are disappointed that when the battery runs out, you have to send your iPod away and pay £85 for a new one. 'That is the reason why many people favour the N91 Jukebox', quoted David Read, the editor of Gadget Magazine.

The N91 will have a memory of 40 gb and will be sold at a launch price of £299.99. The phone will be brought out everywhere, around August 15th, 2005. Further details will be published nearer to the launch date.

Jack Virtue (12)
Fazakerley High School

A Day In The Life Of Eminem

In Eminem's day, he will get up very early in the morning and will go to the shops for an hour or two. Then he will come home and will pack the stuff away. He will have a chill for a while, and then go in his car to the recording studio. Before he goes into the studio, he will sign a few autographs.

He will do some interviews and sing some songs like, 'Mosh', 'Just Lose It', 'Mockingbird' and 'Slim Shady'. Eminem, who has starred in the movie, '8 Mile', is also in a band called D12. His latest CD is called 'Encore'.

After the studio, he goes home and has a sleep. He then gets up and travels to another country or city to prepare for a big concerts. This lasts for five hours.

He then travels home and goes to bed, knowing there will be another hard day ahead of him.

Alan Guyers (12)
Fazakerley High School

Secret Shadows

One day, a girl called Stacey walked down the stairs and saw a funny box she'd never seen before. Her mum said her nan had sent it for her. She looked in it and then she heard someone say, 'Come in.' Stacey thought she couldn't fit in it, but she put her finger in the box and it went very small, so she put her leg in it and it went very small, so she put her body in it too.

She was very scared. It was very dark inside and she'd never done this before. She was so excited when she saw a shadow moving. She thought it must be scared as well, and ran after it, but it jumped out of the box. It was a shadow.

Stacey heard a scream; it was her mum. She followed the shadow out and another shadow too. It was really scary. She heard another scream and she thought it was her mum again, but this time it was her sister.

Stacey wanted to try and get to her mum and sister, but she couldn't find them. She thought they were dread, because she couldn't hear them screaming anymore.

When she saw her mum and sister, they were OK, but then the shadow appeared again.

She said, 'What is the matter?'

The shadow did not reply, but it floated back into the box and it never came back again.

Rebecca Anderson (12)
Fazakerley High School

On The Road To Istanbul

Last night at Anfield two English teams, Chelsea and Liverpool, played for the very first full English Champions League semi-final in its history. The first leg was crucial for both semi-finalists. It ended 0-0, but last night was the final step to Istanbul and Liverpool won it in a surprising 1-0 defeat for Chelsea. The goal came from Luis Garcia, it was a tricky goal to call for, but the referee said goal and that's what counts. After the game, the referee stated that, 'If I never said it was a goal for Liverpool, I would have shown a red card to Petr Cech, plus given a penalty to Liverpool.'

After the game, Rafael Benitez and his team went to the Albert Dock to celebrate the win. Liverpool have won the Champions League four times before. Can they make it five?

Liverpool will play either PSV or AC Milan in the final AC have a 2-0 aggregate lead going into the second leg, but they are away. AC are the favourites to face Liverpool in Istanbul, but can PSV do the impossible as the PSV manager says?

Liverpool are in the final for certain, but are they in next season's Champions League? As it stands Chelsea, Arsenal, Manchester United and Everton will go through and the FA has decided that the top four Premiership teams will go through, even if Liverpool win the Champions League final. The only way they can get through to next season's Champions League is if they get fourth, which will be hard as they have Arsenal and Aston Villa left to play, or if the UEFA let five Premiership teams go through.

Jordan Bennett (12)
Fazakerley High School

A Day In The Life Of An Elephant

I chose this animal mainly because I strongly disagree with the fact that many elephants are being murdered each day so people can use their ivory to make money.

Eyes open slowly, take a look around. Another day in the African bush full of carnivorous creatures and dehydrated plants. I gradually heaved myself up. Edging closer to extinction, most of my kind have died trying to survive without water; others have died due to starvation.

In the distance I could see a great minaret of smoke. I raced across the desert plain towards the now billowing smoke. As I got nearer, I noticed a group of people heading north, away from me. I trumpeted, making for the deserted campsite. The people before me ran in the opposing direction until they were completely out of sight. I marched through the campsite, stamping out the dying embers of a fire left by the humans. Tents flew up rapidly into the polluted air as I moved them only slightly with my trunk.

After time had been spent identifying the objects left by the campers, I decided to make my way back to my family.

Terror! My friends lay dead. Limp. Tusk-less on the floor. Blood seeped into the still water nearby, causing small ripples. The usual poachers had returned. Their figures haunted the past and now they had come to cause more rage! My family had survived! they came out from hiding beneath huge leaves and soldier-like trees that guarded them. Tears streamed down from closed eyes. Lost ones. Never to be seen again ...

Although this unbearable incident seems like a once in a lifetime incident, it wasn't. It was an everyday situation ...

Kelsea Greene (12)
Fazakerley High School

Beeper And Bobulas

Once in the land of Findalue, there was a boy who was 15 years old. He had a mum called Beener, who loved him. One night, lightning struck at Bobulas' house. His mother tried to save him, but tragically died. The gods showed mercy and saved him.

One month later, Bobulas was still sad. Fredulas, a very smart man who lived in the village, told him about the enchanted cup in the Beeper's head. The Beeper was a terrible beast with a flame-thrower on his head, and the strongest legs and arms in the land. If you bled into the cup, one person would be reborn.

Bobulas left in search of the Beeper, scared and weary at the same time, not knowing what would happen and when it would. He was walking for a few days, when he saw it. It was vile and old. Bobulas was the first person to see it in centuries.

The Beeper tried to stay out of sight but Bobulas could still see it. He ran towards the beast and struck, and off came its head. He sliced it in half and got the cup. He ran for his mother's life, keeping her image in his head and heart.

As he got there, the picture faded and he cut himself. Blood poured into the cup and he wished repeatedly, but nothing happened. Outraged, he went to Fredulas and killed him.

That wasn't the end of his life, he lived on thinking of only one thing ... death.

Daniel Burns (12)
Fazakerley High School

Akilleus And Bubbleiseus

Akingeus, king of Athens had a son, but not just any son, he was special. He had amazing strength, and as he grew older, so did his strength. Then one day, his father told him about Bubbleiseus. Akilleus wished him dead and swore an oath to kill him.

Before his journey, his father gave him a sword. 'This sword will destroy anything it touches,' he said. They said their last goodbyes and the Akilleus sailed off in search of the monster.

He sailed past cities and cities, but very strangely the buildings were made out of a pink, gooey material, which you got stuck in if you touched it. Once he met the Bubbeiseus, they didn't even think about chatting, they just went straight into battle.

Bubbleiseus threw his bubble bombs, which turned people into bubblegum, and his close combat weapon was his sword, also made out of bubblegum. The battle lasted for ages, Akilleus matching blow by blow.

Later Bubbleiseus grew tired, so Akilleus struck him blow after blow until he cut his head off. Later on, Akingeus came with the terrible news that Bubbleiseus was his brother! Akilleus was so upset that even the god Zeus felt sorry for him, and so Akilleus ascended to the heavens and became god of strength.

Anthony Lackey (12)
Fazakerley High School

The Papergirl

A long time ago in Smithdown House, the curtains began to move. I had never seen any movement before in this house. I am a papergirl and I have been doing this job for about a year, and since I have, I've never met the person who lives here yet.

One day as I was doing my job, I suddenly heard lots of banging; the door started to open with a creak and I began to get scared. There before me I saw a great big hand with enormous nails; I didn't know what to do. With trembling legs I had to walk in to see what it was. I looked round the door and the door slammed shut. I started to scream, but no one was there. I didn't know who or where this person or creature was.

I could see my breath hanging in the air, it was freezing. *How strange,* I thought.

I walked through to the kitchen and there was a knife lying on the floor, covered with blood. I didn't know where it had come from.

I started to see blood dripping from the ceiling above me. *Drip, drip,* it fell to the floor. My eyes searched the ceiling for clues. At this time I was getting nervous. I was so scared as I walked up the stairs.

As I started to slowly climb the stairs, I heard lots of noise and got the strangest smell I have ever smelt. It smelt like stale blood. I opened the door and there was a puddle of blood. I didn't know what to do, whether to ring the police or carry on looking. I carried on looking.

There was a walk-in wardrobe in the corner of the room. As I walked in, I thought I was going to be sick. There before me were three dead bodies. I started to scream with shock.

I looked more closely. There as a note on one of the bodies, it said, 'I know who you are and I know what you do, if you tell the police, it will happen to you'.

Emma Jones (14)
Fazakerley High School

The Story Of Crusher

There once was a queen called Mary and she was evil. She had a pet monster called Crusher. The queen also had a little boy called Markes, and when he was 12, he one night got drunk so his mum, the queen, kicked him out onto the street the next morning.

One day a man picked him up from the entrance to the palace and asked Markes his name. Markes told him and the man whispered, 'The son of Queen Mary!'

With this, the boy started to cry!

The man took him to his house and told him a story. The story was of the queen, Markes' mum, and how she was so evil, that every thousand years her pet kills all of the city. The next time this would happen would be in five years.

Five years later, Markes heard that Crusher had killed half of the city, so he got prepared. He found his sword and shield and saw Crusher on top of the queen's palace. He climbed up and started to fight him. He swung left to right and then he fell off the building, but hung on.

The monster looked down and Markes threw the sword at his face and Crusher died. Markes climbed back down the palace walls and ran to the nearest hospital.

Markes was fine and the whole city cheered.

Message: be happy with what you have got.

Joseph Finegan (12)
Fazakerley High School

The Mission Of The Creature

Hercules, the son of the king was born. As he grew up he was into sword fighting with his friend Perseus. One day Hercules was fighting with Perseus when suddenly he heard a monster.

Hercules ran to his father telling him that there was a monster in the hill. His father told him that he had seen the monster on the top of the hill for many years. He also said that the monster had killed Hercules' mother many years ago. Hercules decided that when he was older he would kill it.

As the years passed Hercules got older and angrier and when he was 23-years-old, he set off on his mission. As he was walking down the street his best mate ran after him. He said, 'I am coming with you.' They set off on his mission together.

As they were walking up the hill, two wild dogs came out and ran at them. Hercules pulled his sword out and cut their heads off while Perseus ran ahead. Hercules said it was not safe, but Perseus did not listen and a flying sword cut his head off. Hercules had to go on alone.

Hercules ran up to the top of the hill. The monster was waiting and Hercules pulled out his sword and sliced the monster's head off. He ran down the hill to his father with the monster's head and told him that it was all over …

Carl Green (12)
Fazakerley High School

Criptos And Colossus

In the city of Yanokopolis there lived a king and he had a son Criptos. By the age of five he could beat anyone from the whole city in a fight. Criptos felt like a challenge so he went to his father and asked if he could find a better fighter for him.

His dad told him the story of the ferocious beast, Colossus, that many people had gone to fight him and never returned. Criptos said that he would go and challenge Colossus and come back with the head. However he went to fight and was defeated by the beast.

Years passed and Criptos trained and trained and trained, so in the end he became bigger and stronger. Then one day he went to Crete with his mother and father and he saw King Bobasia sacrificing his brother Aries and his sister Athena to Colossus.

Criptos got frustrated and furious with Bobasia and killed him with one quick swoop of his sword. Then took his brother and sister to his father King Monosa and went to fight the beast for a second time, but this time it was to the death.

Days passed and each one, scar by scar. Then eventually Criptos sliced off the head of the brutal beast.

He came back to his city with the head and Criptos became a god, then a king ten years later.

Michael Gibson (12)
Fazakerley High School

The Bus Journey

On the 12th year of the 12th month of the 12th day it gets to eat.

Elsewhere John and his school friends were travelling through the country when a strange-cloaked man ran across the road. The driver stopped, the bus jerked left and right causing Sally, John's friend to scream at the top of her voice. After calming Sally down the driver continued driving.

Later that night, with one hour of the journey left, both tyres on the right burst - yet again the bus jerked. Sally threw-up and everyone had to get off the bus. Whilst waiting, Peter, Sally's boyfriend, was heard screaming and as the scream faded Sally claimed to see Peter in the sky. Everyone moved towards the entrance of the bus when all of a sudden the bus tipped to the right where, described in John's words, 'It took off into the sky with wings longer than a bus, it's horrific screech was heard by all.'

Then Peter came limping down the road shouting, 'Run, it will be back. I am lucky to have broken its grip, don't stand here, run!' An identical screech was heard and it grabbed Peter and killed him.

Everyone ran towards the field. By the time they were at the field it was chasing on the wing. Then a van swerved across the field and a man in the back shot a crossbow at the creature's head, knowing only that it would be back.

Gary Stanley (12)
Fazakerley High School

Kendra And Katrina

When the world was young, a goddess was born. She was beautiful, with blonde ringlets and bright blue eyes. She had the power to apparate. She lived with her brother Marcus and father Zarzon, as she didn't know her mother.

When Katrina was twenty-one, she had a party. She received many presents. However, the thing she wanted most was her mother. She had asked Marcus many times to explain about her, but he normally never said anything. Today he decided she was old enough to know. He told her she was the evil Kendra, who lived in Crete; she was under a spell that could only be lifted if a sword was put through her heart. She decided to apparate to Crete and search every day to find her mother.

One evening she came to a cave. Inside she found her mother. She had stringy hair, sharp claws and fierce eyes.

'Who comes to me?' hissed Kendra.

'It's me ... your daughter, Katrina.'

'I have no daughter,' and Kendra pounced on her with her claws. Before Kendra reached her, Katrina pulled a sword from her belt and plunged it through Kendra's heart. She fell to the floor.

Kendra rose slowly, they looked into each other's eyes then they ran into each other's arms and started crying. Eventually they returned back home.

When her brother and father saw them they celebrated with a party and invited everybody to rejoice. The birthday wish had come true.

Stephanie Bewley (12)
Fazakerley High School

A Day In The Life Of Mrs Hancock

As I sit in my stark white room I hear the dull thud as the slit in my door is opened. The plate of sloppy mashed potatoes with a single meagre sausage that is my evening meal is pushed through. Although evening would suggest that I knew the difference between morning, afternoon and night. Most people would, that is if they hadn't been kept inside for 12 years.

My room for this time has remained as it was the day that I first moved in: bare, lifeless, un-embellished and dismal. For 12 years I have not read a book, watched television, seen my family, looked in a mirror or prepared my own meal.

I did not bring any luggage as I was told that my clothing for my stay would be a white hospital gown. They used the word stay as if I were going to a hotel, for a holiday, to enjoy myself, to relax.

So I have been sitting in my cage, in my zoo with no human contact. I do not remember what my face looks like nor do I remember what my husband's, children's or grandchildren's faces look like. They are faded like characters from a book that I read many years ago and can't quite remember now.

Who knows how long I will be in here for? The rest of my life? When will I finally be able to walk out of these gates and say goodbye to my home, the mental ward.

Heather Nielsen (13)
St Julie's High School, Woolton

A Day In The Life Of Charlie

I knew what day it was. I had been prepared for a while now, and I knew what was coming. I could hear the sound of footsteps marching up and down. I curled up as small as I could go into a ball and crouched down as low as I could so I couldn't be seen. My heart thudded as the barn door opened. They shouted, 'Charlie, Charlie,' but I tried not to flinch. The footsteps continued and they were getting closer. I shut my eyes tightly and hoped that they wouldn't peep around the corner - but they did. I felt two warm hands tickle my belly and I knew I wouldn't get that warm sensation that I felt, for much longer. They took me and put me in the back of the truck and my heart sank - it was all over.

The journey felt like it took forever but sure enough it soon came to an end. I was carried into a pristine white room and laid onto a table. I could see my owner Julie crying and I shut my eyes. Soon after I felt an unbearable pain in my back and my whole life flashed before my eyes. Then slowly I felt myself drift into a heavy sleep and that was it - all over.

Alexandra Hughes (13)
St Julie's High School, Woolton

A Day In The Life Of Jack Cornwall

The lure of the room was strong. I knew important things went on in there, a mere page shouldn't have gone in, but I just had to take a peek.

'Ah, there you are!' boomed Sir John Coldicot, one of King Arthur's closest friends. I assumed he needed the round table cleaned!

'I have a job for you,' said Sir John assumingly.

'Yes Sir,' I tentatively replied.

'I need you to take this to the King, he's on the battlefield. Let no one know who you are, nor get their hands on the message.'

I shouldn't have accepted, this would be a huge step from a simple page to a brave messenger.

I ran as fast as I could, but quickly thought I would be less conspicuous if I walked.

It took me most of the day to reach the battleground. I was nearly compromised as I passed through evil Baron Trumph's territory, I had to dodge and creep to remain unseen. When I reached the battleground, I had to crawl through the corpses but miraculously managed to reach the King unharmed.

Instead of crawling through the crossfire on the way back, I decided to walk with a stoop. I became increasingly confident.

This really is the right job for me, I said to myself. I challenged myself to stand, proud to be the King's messenger, I was stupid, I felt a sharp pain in my back. Why can't I catch my breath? This can't be happening, I'm just a page!

Amy Bennett (13)
St Julie's High School, Woolton

The Kelpie

I tiptoed across the soft damp grass and shuffled my way through the thick piles of rotten autumn leaves that lay still on the floor, and smelt the foul odour that lifted as I disturbed them.

I finally reached the pond that lay in the middle of the wood. I stared deep into its murky waters, hoping to catch a glimpse of what I was searching for. I knew the risks that I was taking. Yet I stayed standing at the muddy edge of the pond, my camera clutched in my hands. The night was young. Minutes passed and I began to feel impatient. I was beginning to wonder whether I should go, when the water began to bubble.

I could not believe my eyes. A black horse was rising from the water, as if it was being created from it.

It strode towards me and knelt down. I knew what this was. It was what I had been searching for. It was the kelpie. Its white eyes stared into mine. I felt them creep further, going into my mind, as if they were hypnotising me. Suddenly I found myself walking towards the kelpie. I dropped my camera. I mounted the evil spirit. I had no control. The kelpie rose with me on its back, and walked into the pond. I clung to its soft mane, and closed my eyes. I felt water slowly climb its way up my body. I felt cold. Then I felt nothing.

Samantha Brennan (13)
St Julie's High School, Woolton

A Day In The Life Of A Five Pound Note

So here I am, again! Back in the cold, dark, claustrophobic conditions of a shop till. Light! The till is being opened, finally! The shop assistant passes me into an old wrinkly hand, its owner, a pensioner puts me in their moth-eaten, old purse. It must be a woman, there is a heavy scent of lavender surrounding her, almost like a cloud.

While I have been thinking, my 'new home' has been put into a bag and thrown around, probably down to the quick pace this lady is walking at. She's fast for an elder! This rocking is making me tired, I think I'll catch some *Zzzzzz* ...

What! Oh, the old dear has stopped. She's taking out her purse. She's opened the purse and is fishing around for her keys. Suddenly there is a huge gust of wind. I can feel myself being lifted up, up and away. I'm free! No more stuffy purses! Goodbye cold shop tills. Nothing can stop me now! I can feel the wind dropping now. I'm floating slowly and steadily to the ground. The floor is wet.

Give me a purse anyday, compared to this. There's not much I can do to help myself now, so I think I'll catch up on my beauty sleep ...

Well that was a good nap ... where am I? It's warm ... I must be in someone's pocket. Watch where you're putting your hand! I'm being exchanged for something, can't see what ...

So here I am, again! Back in the cold, dark, claustrophobic conditions of a shop till ...

Chloe Pettit (14)
St Julie's High School, Woolton

A Day In The Life Of It

Why? Why me? What have I done wrong? Every moment that I'm alive, I'm sure is a moment nearer my death.

My life has been like this for as long as I can remember. The hunger ... the tears ... the excuses ... the blood ... the fist!

I used to sit in the corner of a room praying. I would pray that God would take me away from this life, I soon realised He didn't care about me either. I have come to terms with this but I still wonder why? Why me?

My future years are predictable, they will no doubt be filled with hatred, blood and suffering.

I like to sit in the open field behind my house. There I can clear my mind, forget about the bruises that cover my body like a swarm of bees covering a hive.

Some days I imagine what it would be like to be loved. How I long for this feeling. They always say I'm a day-dreamer and if I do it in front of them they will put me in my place. I can't help day-dreaming. It is my way of escaping their bloody hands.

I have an old teddy bear who comforts me in my long, lonely days. Sometimes I talk to him, I even ask him questions because I love him that much that I think he's real. But in the end I know he's not.

I ask him why? Why me? But there's no answer.

Zoë Nolan (13)
St Julie's High School, Woolton

The Woman On The Stairs

'The doorknob slowly turned, the door flew open. Tom fell over in shock. He walked over to the door and looked down the stairs. A small, old woman was at the bottom. She looked up and grinned at Tom. She started to crawl up the stairs, her hair falling out as she did. Her skin was green and rotten. She'd been dead for years. Tom ran back to his room and locked the door.

'Tom, let me in darling. I won't hurt you!' cried a creepy voice from the other side of the door.

'Leave me alone,' Tom cried, tears streaming down his face.

The woman had been after Tom for years, ever since he vandalised her grave. She started scratching against the door. Suddenly the door flew open. Tom tried to yell but nothing came out.

'It's OK child, I won't hurt you, come with me and you can be my child forever,' said the woman.

'No, I'll never go!'

The woman got closer and closer, her eyes gleaming, she was smiling, showing her rotten yellow teeth. Getting so close that Tom could feel her breath on his cheeks ...

'What happens next?' Alex asked eagerly.

'I don't know, I haven't thought of it yet!' said Jack.

They were in Alex's room, having a sleepover. Suddenly the doorknob turned and the door flew open. No one was there. They both jumped.

As Alex went to shut the door he heard the stairs creaking. No one else was in the house. As he looked down the stairs he yelled and stepped back in shock ...

The police are still investigating the disappearance of Alex Smith and Jack Hunter. All the evidence the police found were scratches on Alex's bedroom door and grey hair on the stairs.

Rachael McPaul (14)
St Julie's High School, Woolton

The Ghost Dog

As the sun rose on the early Thursday morning an eerie feeling was fleeing across Liverpool. Caroline went regularly for a refreshing morning walk. Muffins had been her dog whom she cherished and loved dearly. Unfortunately Muffins had died last year and the pet's anniversary had come back round. On the same day its owner would die too.

The clock ticked slowly, every minute lasting a lifetime. Caroline, unsure what to do with herself as her morning walk would remind herself of the animal she once named Muffins. Bored to death, she decided to pull herself together and visit the park to relive some happy memories that couldn't be returned.

Stepping slowly down the long and winding road listening to the birds singing softly, the bright sun beat down as though saying hello. However, for Caroline some happiness would be found on this day.

The park's entrance finally approached her, already tears were growing but something was ordering Caroline to go on. Entering the park felt like being in a time machine as past memories surrounded her. Her head to the ground as though witnessing a funeral procession. At this point a rather peculiar incident happened. There was a barking in the clearance. It sounded as though it was being whispered. Memories of Muffins returned. The bark's volume began to increase and the night was drawing to an end. There was no one around, no one except Muffins, no Caroline and no life left inside her.

Charlotte Williams (13)
St Julie's High School, Woolton

A Day In The Life Of Katy Sony

I can't say I wasn't warned. Adverts about it were all over the television and every person told me to do it when I got into a car. But I ignored them. So every time I went out in 'my friend's' car (it wasn't, but so what, and he wasn't old enough to drive but he's cool) I never fastened my seat belt (even when he was drunk), I'd never got hurt and I believed I never would.

I've just been for a ride with my friends, but I'm standing on the pavement (I don't know how though). I watched a body being covered up and put on a stretcher and into an ambulance.

'Is that everyone?' the ambulance driver asked his colleague.

'No,' I said, stepping into the ambulance.

'Yes,' replied the person in the ambulance, 'you can drive now.'

During the ride no one asked me how I was, but then again the girl on the trolley was dying. At the hospital, everyone sped off and left me to wander around. I kept asking people where to go but they were in a rush and never seemed to hear me. Then I heard a nurse tell a doctor my family had arrived. They walked into a room, so I followed only to find my family crying over my body. My body? It hit me, I was the girl on the trolley ... I was dead.

Natalie Edwardson (13)
St Julie's High School, Woolton

A Day In The Life Of Isaac Goldstein

Being who I am or my 'type' as they say, I've no guaranteed quality or length of life.

Everything is a bad surprise, the reasons are unpredictable and the actions are unforgettable.

We heard them marching down our streets of Warsaw. As my mother heard this, she began to tidy, clean and hide away any visible valuables. She spoke in utter fear and vulnerability when she said, 'They're on their way. Behave for the Germans now children, they have their reasons.' She, of course, knew that these reasons were wrong and inexcusable, but she knew she couldn't argue with their rules. My sister Helen, however was not so fearful.

When we heard the sudden fire of a Nazi gun, Helen, after being told not to, put her head out of the window and saw a horrifying sight. It was her best friend Danka, shot in cold blood. After seeing that, she couldn't help but shout out, 'Murderers, Murderers!' and then of course, she faced the consequences. At that moment, the Nazi soldier who shot Danka shot my sister. At first, it was a quick flash, but then it was a brutal act of evil in slow motion. I felt a sudden increase in weight on my feet. She had fallen on me. My dead sister was bleeding at my feet and there was nothing I could do about it.

I know that many more people have and will die in this awful nightmare, but for me, this one event is what the Holocaust is all about. I pray every night that this will go away. 'It's never too late,' my mother says, but I am beginning to doubt that it will ever end, and if it does will I make it? Will I live to tell the story?

Sarah Jones (13)
St Julie's High School, Woolton

The Warning

The other night I was sitting on the couch. I heard a lot of noise outside.

I went outside, nothing or no one there.

I came back in and I put on a scary DVD, it sounded like someone was running up and down the stairs.

I walked slowly up the stairs and no one was there, but in my room I heard something, I went down and a cold shiver ran down my spine.

The DVD was all blurry, like it had gone off channel. I stepped on the remote and the DVD was still on. I sat back down and watched the DVD but dozed off. I woke up in a fright, freezing. My blinds were blowing everywhere. I shut the window and got a bit scared wondering why the window was wide open in the first place.

I went into the kitchen to put the heating on and get a drink. I walked back into the living room and sat down. I put the TV on a random channel and put my feet up and saw a shadow in the corner of my eye. It came in and sat down on the couch, I thought I was dreaming.

The next day I went over to the housing office and asked who used to live there.

The man said, 'An old married couple lived there, the husband, he killed his wife and is now looking for her and peace.'

Gemma Hill (13)
St Julie's High School, Woolton

A Day In The Life Of Billy The Beggar

It was just an ordinary day for me, I woke up as per usual, with the cold shivering up my spine and my head tingling from the coldness of the pavement slabs I lay on. As I sat up and looked at the happenings around me, I stopped, and thought for a moment about the challenges that lay ahead of me. My stomach began to talk to me as I thought about where I would get my meal from today. I began on my never-ending journey to find scraps of food.

After rummaging through the rubbish bins, and finding only a half-eaten banana, which by the way was the only edible thing in the bins, I decided I would not go to my spot where I go usually and beg, just around the corner from the bakers, but I would go onto the bridge. You see, here more people pass, therefore probably I will end up with more money and more food. What a treat that would be. So off I went.

Just sitting here doing nothing is so boring you know, I suppose I only have myself to blame. If only I hadn't got into that argument with my stepdad, I probably would be there with them all eating and having fun in the warm and in a place where I would be loved, but oh no, I had to open my big mouth and here I am in the cold and with nobody around me who loves me, and with no food or money. It must be at least two months now since I've had a proper meal, I have lost lots of weight, in fact so much that every bone in my body sticks out of my ripped clothes, and that my skin is almost transparent, but I have to be strong for myself, and just get on with life, because I know it will be over soon.

'Any spare change please?'

'Please?'

'Any spare change please?'

As I sit here shouting this at the top of my voice, using all the energy I have left, I just stopped for a moment and listened to all the comments those *perfect* people made about me.

'Scruff.'

'Dirty beggar.'

'Tramp.'

'Rat.'

With those words running through my mind one after the other after the other, I just lay on the cold, damp floor, and began to try and cry myself to sleep hoping everything would be alright.

Just lying there made me think of all the weather and dangerous positions my life has made me face. I just want it to be over.

'Please someone put me out of my misery, please Lord let me be out of pain, out of danger, and out of the cold once and for all. It may sound terrible, but help me to end my life in some way or another. Help me please, help me ...'

Rachel Chandler (14)
St Julie's High School, Woolton

Outcast

As I sat on the cliff edge, overlooking the bay, I watched as the waves rolled over the shore and took tiny grains of sand and shells back to the sea. It reminded me of my life. The waves were the people each taking a grain of sand, each grain of sand was a piece of me, a memory, a smile, a tear.

I was alone in the world. My heart felt as though it had an anchor wrapped around it, it was sinking, deeper and deeper into the depths of my unhappiness. I had seen the way they looked at me in school, the way they laughed. I had tried so hard to fit in, but I was never going to be a part of the crowd, I was always going to be an outcast.

My best friend, was the one true friend I had, but we went to different schools. She was fun and exciting. She enjoyed her life, enjoyed school, she was popular, she fitted in, she was part of the crowd. I longed to go to her school, I longed to be friends with her friends, to speak to someone every day, instead of standing alone on the playground and sitting alone at lunch.

I woke up each day with a feeling of dread in the pit of my stomach. There was no way out, I convinced myself, no possible way to overcome my self-torture. I fingered the compass that lay in my pocket, I could feel the sharp point against my fingertips. I placed it against my wrist, *you can do it,* I told myself.

You do realise what you're about to do don't you? a voice said, *imagine what will happen if you just move that compass across your skin. What you'll put your family through.*

I felt a warmth wash over me, I realised what I was doing, I knew it was wrong. I stood on the cliff edge and threw the compass onto the beach. I watched as the waves took the compass into the depths of the deep, this was another portion of my life which was taken, a portion I longed to forget.

Lauren Curtis (14)
St Julie's High School, Woolton

Growing Up

Growing up, turning from a child into a woman, things change and why? Who knows! You can't have a free mind, with no problems hassling you. I wish I were a child again, like in the olden days, no worries about relationships or the way you look. Just free to enjoy seeing things and learning.

Everyone always says, 'Ooh aren't you growing up fast?' You just smile and laugh but when you deeply think about it you realise that your childhood is really flying past you. You should never wish to be older than you actually are as it soon approaches.

Days turn into months, months turn into years and years fly past so quickly, it feels like a moment. Your attitude becomes more serious, maturity takes place and you start to think before you act. Foolishness and fantasies disappear. You grow up in a make-believe world bestowed upon you by your parents. Believing in the Tooth Fairy and Father Christmas when you are young fills you with excitement, but when beliefs start to fade away you still appreciate special events but not as much.

Protection of the real world from your parents comes to a halt and you start to acknowledge what independence and the real world is like.

You wonder what your future will hold and what your life will be like as you realise it's sooner than you think. You want to fulfil your dreams of a perfect house etc but you understand it might never happen.

Why can't time stop and everything stay the same? I suppose that will never happen and in the mean time live your childhood to the full and never waste a day!

Clare Bowman (14)
St Julie's High School, Woolton

Finally Over

The dust settled on the quiet neighbourhood; the screams had long since faded away. The houses that were left stood amongst the rubble of the ones that had got in the way.

All the pain and suffering was over and across the country, men, women and children celebrated the victory.

Down the street, people started to emerge from their empty houses, into the silent world. Smiles spread across the once gloomy faces, and children broke free of their parents' grasps knowing they were once again safe. Friends and relatives embraced each other and praised the Lord that they had survived.

Laughter broke through the air and overcame the tears that had taken over for such a long time.

Everyone anxiously awaited the return of their heroes; the return of their husbands, fathers and sons.

Suddenly, a loud bang echoed across the street; but this time it was not the sound of destruction but of celebration. Fireworks. Red, green, blue, gold and silver stars filled the sky, as people below clapped and cheered at the amazing display.

The celebrations went through long into the night. There was not one single person who wasn't either rejoicing the triumph or remembering those lost in the struggle.

It was not the time to forgive and move on as normal. And the time to forget about the past and think about the future.

The war was over.

Rebecca Seaman (14)
St Julie's High School, Woolton

A Day In The Life Of A Cancer Patient

Every day I watch from my window. I watch all the children just like me playing, but they aren't just like me. I have leukaemia.

I knew as soon as the doctor opened the door to the waiting room. All those years of training just to tell someone that they won't live till their next birthday.

So those kids outside my window, they are normal. They can look forward to their 18th birthdays, getting their first car, getting married, but all I have to look forward to is sitting in this claustrophobic room for days on end getting drugs that will only prolong the time I spend there.

I hate it, I hate not knowing whether I will wake up the next morning, I hate the throwing up and not having hair, I hate just watching.

I'm an outsider. People are afraid to look me in the eye. It's not just children, adults too. They think it's better not to say anything but give fake smiles when I can see it, pity in their eyes.

I'm not one of these people who are an inspiration and are brave and achieve everything within the few months they're given. I don't even feel able to lift a cup, let alone run a marathon.

I just want it to come quickly. I'm not afraid, I've been through too much pain to be scared. All I ask is for it to come sooner rather than later.

Sophie Hyland (14)
St Julie's High School, Woolton

The Circus

Last night was amazing. Nana and Grandad took me to the circus for my birthday.

They picked me up at around five-thirty after school. As I got into their car Mum and Dad shouted, 'Have a good time!'

As we were driving there, I was getting a strange sensation in my stomach, as if someone was squeezing it. Nana said it was nerves.

We eventually got there and were shown to our seats with our candyfloss. I was staring inquisitively at the huge red curtain waiting for the show to begin. The lights went dim. The strange sensation came back in my stomach.

'Hoorah!' everybody shouted as the colourful clowns entered the ring. They were wearing fluorescent yellows and royal blues. They were very silly, shoving pies in each other's faces and tripping each other up.

Next came the acrobats. They were amazing, in their matching glittery costumes which glistened in the spotlights. They swung from rope to rope, balanced themselves in all sorts of unusual positions and walked across the tightropes. Grandad said this was his favourite part.

There were very unusual men there, who had really long legs and were juggling with flaming batons. I didn't see what was so special about these because Nana can juggle with oranges.

Lastly came the ringmaster with a magnificent roaring lion that was at least twice the size of him. Everything seemed to go into slow motion as the lion leapt through flaming rings of fire to end the show.

What a night!

Nicola Allen (13)
St Julie's High School, Woolton

Miss Nobody

I sat in my corner of the playground, the corner where nobody sat. That's what I am see, nobody; just the four-eyed freak, who everyone thinks it's already to bully - well not anymore. Gemma and her twisted two-faced gang can find someone else to pick on. I've had more than my share of their bullying and it's about time they knew it!

As I sat confidently and unthreatened, I caught a glimpse of the queen wolf and her pack, following closely behind her. Aware that they were going to confront me, I stood up, still feeling confident and assured.

Suddenly she appeared right in front of me. I was becoming smaller and smaller; well that's what it felt like. She had that effect on people! Nevertheless, I held my head up high, as I was to be the one person to stand up to the most popular girl at school, even if I was Miss Nobody!

I thought I would give her the chance to be the humiliated one for a change! I thought wrong!

My heart skipped a beat as she approached me. I couldn't breathe properly. I opened my mouth but no words escaped. I started stuttering and mumbling but they just laughed in my face, like I was an animal in the zoo. I could feel my eyes filling up. I wanted to just break down there and then, but I knew that it would only cause me more humiliation.

Instead, I flooded the toilets with tears. They were uncontrollable, they just continually poured out as if someone had left the tap on.

Afterwards I returned to my 'nobody' corner, my undesirable reality!

Victoria Simms (14)
St Julie's High School, Woolton

A Day In The Life Of A Death Camp Victim

It's nearly my turn to see the gentlemen at the front of the queue. It had been an awfully long wait. The sun has risen and set a good number of times whilst I've been waiting in this line. The heavens have opened up twice leaving the passengers drenched as if we have swum in a lake, but it cleansed us of our thirstiness which has been troubling us for the past two days, whilst being crammed into the vans. It will all be worth it in the end I suppose, for my daughter and me. The kind gentleman that picked us up promised us we were being sent to a better place, where we would be looked after properly away from the commotion of the city. Maybe we will see my husband who was sent out a few months ago to work in the country. I told him to write but maybe it got lost in the post.

Although relieved we are nearly there, I am also a little frightened but I don't want my fear to show to Emily. I have to be strong for her and hold her hand as the world has flown past her within a couple of days. I have seen a couple of mothers and their children being sent into buildings of some sort and they have not yet returned. They will be out soon enough and then it will be Emily's and my turn. But my patience is beginning to turn to suspense and from suspense to fear.

Oh well it's our turn now. Wish us luck.

Jynell Murphy (14)
St Julie's High School, Woolton

They Had It Coming

It didn't happen. It's not me sitting here with my head in my hands. It's not real; it's not. I repeat this desperately, trying to convince myself that I am sane and what I just did; did not occur.

I raise my fifth glass of red wine to my lips, drinking in deeply, washing down the trials and tribulations of my life. At least that's what I pretend to do. I catch sight of myself in the mirror across the room, the wine glimmers like blood on my lips morphing me from a self loathing wreck, to a savage revenant licking the 'blood' off my mouth with glee.

I laugh at the irony of my 'life'. A mere week ago I was a successful marriage counsellor with an Adonis of a fiancé on my arm, now I sit perched on a bathtub, drunk beyond belief with blood tinting my fingertips. I try and wash it off, but it remains just as ruby-red and evident as when it first spilt. I become frantic, cursing my hand until my own blood starts to stain it. I throw myself to the ground, sobbing uncontrollably. I can't think straight, I can't even see straight. The bathtub doubles before my eyes and I find myself swigging the dregs of wine straight from the bottle. Sweet intoxication sweeps the dark veil of sleep across my face and I find myself reliving the nightmare of this evening.

I remember the tiresome shift I had that evening, I also remember throwing open my bedroom door to find my fiancée tangled in some blonde. At this point I shudder from sleep, dazed, drenched in cold sweat. A smile plays on my lips and I remind myself: they had it coming.

Zoë Braimah (14)
St Julie's High School, Woolton

A Day In The Life Of A Dog

I still remember the day he picked me out. Me. He could have chosen any of my brothers or sisters but Benji had chosen me. I was so proud as he carried me out, but I was sad too. I knew I would never see my family again, but now I had a new family.

Benji was only four at the time. He was my best friend. We did everything together. Played ball, went for long runs, we even ate our meals together. I hated it when he started school. I lay on his bed all day and as soon as I heard his footsteps on the path I dashed like lightning down the stairs and waited. Mum always took forever to open the door, but when she finally did I was there and we were together again.

Things started to change though, as Benji got older, he had other friends, lots of them. We no longer played ball, he hated running and he said I was too big to get on his bed.

Then he moved out. It was so quiet without him. No sound of drums pounding down the stairs, no doors slamming after an argument, no laughter.

He hardly ever visited, but today he came. Yes, today he came and took me in his car.

I could make out the tears lining his eyes in the mirror from my backseat. Then we arrived. He carried me into the grey, steely room. Cold room. Hardly any light. He whispered something in my ear as he stroked my head ever so gently. Then a man entered with a huge needle. Now the tears flowed freely. I saw a bright light, then ...

Jade Wardell (14)
St Julie's High School, Woolton

Torture In The Mansion

As I stepped inside the cold, dark mansion I heard a piercing sound, a sound that could only be described as blood-curdling screams, coming from the mouths of tortured victims. More screams filled the room, my head spinning, like a whirlwind, spinning faster and faster, I hit the floor.

As I woke it was, I think the next day, as there was just a little light beaming from a tiny crack in the wall. I started to panic, where was I? Yesterday I was stepping inside the mansion and now I am here, chained to a wall. There is no escape, what am I going to do now?

As I turned my head, I noticed a familiar face, my friend who, as well as me, was chained to a wall. I hadn't seen her for days, she had gone missing. The last time anyone saw her, she was walking through the grand gates of the mansion. I suddenly thought to myself, *How long had I been here, unconscious chained to a wall? Nobody knows, will anyone ever know?*

In the corner of the room there was something hiding in the shadows of the murky dungeon of the old mansion. That something came slowly out of the shadows, what was it? Could it be a man or a woman? Or was it just something unnatural, something that could never be explained? It was holding a knife. Slash, there was a big gash in her stomach, she was coughing, it was getting louder and louder. The sharp blade was pushed into her heart. I was stunned in silence, knowing I was going to suffer the same fate. Then darkness ...

Nicola Keen (14)
St Julie's High School, Woolton

First Day

My first day at school, except this day normally comes when the kid is still a young baby, say maybe three or four, but no, good old Elizabeth Walters had to be different. You see, I'm sixteen years of age, and until now I've been home schooled. It's my parents' fault! I've been travelling around the world with them ever since I could say the word 'dada', and now that I am going through the hardest years of my teenage life, they decide to drop me into high school!

My dad dropped me off outside my new school in our banger of a van, which attracted some unwanted attention because of the balls of smoke and toxic fumes coming from the rusty exhaust. I slammed the car shut, nearly taking it off its hinges.

I could feel my neck burning up as passers-by glared at me. I mean it wasn't as if it was my first day of school ... well, it was, but they didn't know that! I looked curiously around the open grounds of the school and at all the pupils, and then I realised. I knew why I stood out like a sore thumb! All these girls were dressed so smartly and lady-like in their tartan kilts and spotless white shirts, apart from one person, me of course! My stupid, idiotic, hopeless parents had forgotten to even buy me a uniform! This really was going to be the worst day I'd ever have.

Melanie Brown
St Julie's High School, Woolton

On My Own

It's almost been five months now. Five long, painful months without you. Each day no easier than the previous. It's like a never-ending circle of sorrow and grief that I'm helplessly trapped in.

I knew that birthdays would be the hardest without you to blow out your share of the candles. Blowing fourteen out all by myself is going to be hard. I don't know if I can do it. I don't know if I can do anything anymore.

My whole life it's been the two of us. Everything came in two. We were a two. Everything you did, I did. But now I feel like I'm slowly deteriorating and crumbling before my very own eyes. I can't be me without you.

I wake up every morning in the hope of seeing you, but all I see is an empty bed beside me. It's all so surreal. One minute we were together then the next we were separated for which so far feels like forever. I feel like I am the one struggling the most in coping with your loss. I try to be strong and pretend that I'm okay for your sake and Mum's and Dad's but the truth is - I'm not.

Words can't express how much you mean to me sister. Sometimes, I wish that I hadn't have been so close to you. But deep down, I know that it's better to have loved and lost than to have never loved at all.

Lauren Machin (14)
St Julie's High School, Woolton

Hide-And-Seek

Why on earth was I here? I can't believe I agreed. Now look at me, my clothes are torn and dirty, I was pouring with sweat and my mood was foul.

The shed was cramped and claustrophobic, the smell of damp wood filled my nose, I could hear birds chirping outside. My legs were aching from the position I was squashed in, the light that came from the crack in the wood shone onto a huge spider in the corner of the shed.

Hearing a noise from outside I froze, I could her the blood pounding in my head. Crawling forward towards the door, I opened it and peered out. Looking out, I saw someone who was searching, searching for me.

Retreating back in the safety of the shed, I heard voices, they hadn't found me. That meant it began again. I started shivering, I was cold, it was warm outside but I was cold inside the shed.

As I sat back on the boxes and sacks that I had been sat on, I stumbled, knocking over a tool box. I stood frozen in my spot praying that I hadn't been heard. Nobody came so I assumed that I hadn't, sitting back on the boxes I once again began to shiver.

Then I once again heard the voice I had been dreading, but this time it was closer.

'Ready or not, here I come.'

Hearing these words, one thought ran through my mind. I hate hide-and-seek.

Nicola Hussey (14)
St Julie's High School, Woolton

What Had Happened To Me?

'Don't do it Lauren,' Jess repeatedly said to me. I was ignoring her now. I knew I had to do it. Why should I carry on living? Nothing was worth it anymore. I hated my life. I hated my mum and dad so much. Just because they had caught me smoking and drinking they had grounded me. But I just had to go, I couldn't carry on any longer.

Suddenly I got an urge and ran, I heard Jess mumbling in the background. A car hit me. All of a sudden I felt strange, my body had shut down, it was just my mind that was still alive.

Was I finally going to go to Heaven? My life would be brilliant. Finally I could be happy. Free.

Suddenly pictures in my mind of my freedom had vanished. I heard voices. I still couldn't work out where they were coming from. When I tried to speak no words would come out. My eyes began to squint and adjust to the bright room. Then I opened them. All around me were strange looking people in white clothing.

Then I saw my mum, she was stroking my hair gently, and saying something to me, but I just couldn't hear what she was saying. What was wrong with me?

Then all of a sudden there was a sound. I could make some words out in my right ear. No, it couldn't be, it couldn't happen to me. I wanted to die but now, for the rest of my life, I would be paralysed.

Lauren Bruce (14)
St Julie's High School, Woolton

A Day In The Life Of An SS Trooper

Every day I do this. Every day I wake from the hair mattress. Every day I see them, arriving, not knowing what I know. I forced myself into this; it's not my fault. I became one of Hitler's dreaded SS troops. I can't do it. It pains me but it's them or me.

I am not the type of person, who just sits there and lets everyone die because they are different, but I have to, that is what I have to do; I have to live with so many deaths on my conscience. Internal pain is unbearable. Other SS troops think it's a laugh. I join in with them, laughing and joking, but inside I think they can see through me. My eyes look fake, I know myself. However I follow the crowd, like the people coming here do.

Every day I see them. Arriving by cattle truck, bruised, battered; they're devoid of energy. They are sorted into lines, to watch it's so degrading. The frail, the old, the young, the Jews, the male and female, the list never-ending. They think they're going to be safe until the war ends. Wrong! I yearn to tell that a death, which is too brutal to comprehend, is closer than ever. Everyone smiles, saying we will be safe - we will be free when the war is over. They will be free but differently - their souls will go to Heaven - Hitler's will rot in the pits of Hell.

I can't bear it anymore, my gun used for the death of other people who are just different, is the only thing that can save me, my soul and set me free from all this pain. It's not them this time, it's me.

Bang!

Ellis Johnson (14)
St Julie's High School, Woolton

A Day In The Life Of A Jew

My name is Suzie, I'm eight, I live in Germany and I am a Jew. Under Hitler's new rules we have been treated differently recently, but Mum said life will soon be back to normal.

Today I was at school and my friend Mary ignored me, I wondered why and asked her why she wasn't my friend, Mary told me she wasn't allowed to because her parents didn't like me anymore.

After school I went into the local sweet shop as usual but the shopkeeper ignored me and told me she wasn't going to serve me, there are shops everywhere now where other girls and boys like me aren't allowed to go in. Mummy says we aren't allowed to go in some because people are different to us and don't like any people who are different, I told Mummy I didn't feel like I was any different to other people and she told me I wasn't but we believed in different things to others.

I have these stars sewn onto my clothes that I can't pick off, Mummy says they are to show people what we believe in but they make people look at me, I don't think anyone likes me anymore, the neighbours don't talk to my family and people always frown at me in the street. I also heard Daddy talking the other day about how his shop isn't getting as many customers as usual, he said this was because of Hitler, Mum said it would be over one day and I hope it will be because I don't like being different, different to other people.

Sophie Doig (14)
St Julie's High School, Woolton

A Day In The Life Of A Cat

I padded the welcoming fuzzy tapestry, feeling the delicious sensation of fur beneath my paws. How wonderful it was to know the day was mine, lulling me ahead to snoozing under the lazy shadow of the elm tree and snuggled up aside the sizzling incandescence of the fireplace. My razor claws glinted beside the flames, fondling the rug, ever prowling for a relaxing position. Tickling my handsome nose, I watched in sheer admiration as my wiry whiskers tingled with each rumbling purr.

Sharply, my ears pricked hearing the somewhat familiar drone of vehicles in the drive and with a swift, graceful bound, I abandoned my snug spot and slid out, a blur of smoky grey fur amongst the red and white paint of the antiquated mahogany door.

A tender smile, an affectionate purr, the rising scent of my companion's returning. Awakened by the cold, hard sensation of paving beneath talons, I slinked between feet and brushed against legs, humming my summertime tune as I went, winding an invisible path like a train travelling a long awaited tunnel.

The day passed with hopes fulfilled, a plate of crisp, steaming cod, the soothing aroma of the family rising in the warmth as I lay in my favourite cosy spot, the drawer above the heater. Letting my tail hang freely, the pleasurable sensation of hot air blowing through wisps of my silvery moonshine fleece, aroused, my eyes closing upon the image of the young girl sitting in the old comfy armchair, her soft, delicate hand reaching out to feel the comforting heat of my body under her hand.

Janine Seddon (14)
St Julie's High School, Woolton

Guilty

'We find the defendant guilty,' said a smartly dressed woman.

I felt numb inside, I began to shake as a policeman handcuffed me. Faye, my so-called friend smirked and gave a sly wave as she forced open the heavy glass doors, laughing hysterically.

'Excuse me, I think a mistake has been made, I haven't done anything wrong!' I sobbed.

However, I could tell by his face that I couldn't say anything now to make things better. He thought I was nothing, scum. He looked at me as if I was something he'd scraped off the bottom of his shoe.

I had nobody now, Faye had managed to turn everyone against me, even my own mother. I'd been convicted for a crime I didn't commit, Faye did. I told her not to drive that car, she'd had way too much to drink. I only let her because I thought it would make me popular, hanging out with someone who was really tough.

She told me to swap seats with her when the police came, she'd said that otherwise they'd arrest her for drink-driving. It was only when the policewoman came up to the window that I realised there was something else, the policewoman told me that this car had been involved in a hit and run. Consequently, she arrested me and Faye told everyone it was true and they believed her.

So now, I'm sitting in a horrible, claustrophobic, filthy room with other youth offenders. I'm sitting with murderers when my only crime is that I wanted to be popular. It's only now that I realise to be popular is totally overrated.

Catherine Handley (14)
St Julie's High School, Woolton

A Day In The Life Of A Doormat

I hold my breath as I hear quiet footsteps in the distance. The front door seems to open in slow motion and I dread the thought of things to come. My whole body becomes tense.

They don't know what it's like, you see. To be trampled on and taken for granted day after day. I didn't ask for it to be this way ...

The front door finally opens and a herd of children pile their way in. Their damp shoes leave raindrops on my skin and the mud dries and hardens, which leaves a terrible stench.

My only pleasure in this meaningless life is my once-a-week trip to the washing machine. It is the only time when I can relax and socialise with others of my kind, those who know what it's like to be me.

Take Jim for instance. To those humans he was known as the back door mat. We were like brothers, me and him, we stuck to each other, no matter what. Then, one awful day, without warning, Jim disappeared. He wasn't in the weekly wash. We suspect that he was thrown into the rubbish. My heart sank when I heard the news. Outside, the heavens opened and the rain poured as if there was no tomorrow.

Then I realised that my life did have some meaning. I was responsible for the cleanliness of their house. This made me feel important, as if I was on a special mission. And to this day, I still sit on the wooden floor of the hall, waiting and listening, for the footsteps in the distance ...

Rachel Holmes (14)
St Julie's High School, Woolton

Icy Breath!

My imagination was running wild; I crept up the stairs, knowing I was alone.

I got to my bedroom safely, reached for the light and heard a *boom!* There was a power cut - I grabbed my torch.

I heard a male voice calling a name, 'Jane ...' I felt breathing on the back of my neck and saw the icy breath sweep across my face. *He* started shouting, 'Jane ...!' It seemed to me *he* was shouting to me.

He stood behind me, grasped my mouth tightly, dragging me into a different realm, dumping me into a dark room, locking me in.

I sat for days, shivering in the room where the daylight never shone. I came up with an idea about how to escape the room. The guard was asleep, leaning against the door with the keys in his pocket poking through the gap under the door; I decided that he would feel me trying to take the key off the bunch, so I took my clip out of my hair and opened the door. I gently pushed it open to see if the guard was still there. He wasn't, so I went through.

I appeared back in my room, boarded my bedroom wall up so *he* couldn't get back through. My mum was just coming through the door; I had been away for more than half an hour.

Now we live elsewhere, but the experience still haunts me after all these years.

Kate Farrell (13)
St Julie's High School, Woolton

Footsteps Are Following ...

My head thumped and my heart raced, my legs ached as I ran through the dark, wooded graveyard. The cold raindrops danced down my face and the wind wildly whistled down my ears.

Why? Why had I taken this shortcut? Why hadn't I gone the usual way home? Why had I split up from my friends? Suddenly for a second the moonlight drenched me in its bright silver light, but darkness showered back over me as I ran beneath the trees.

My fear was now greater than ever as the footsteps that had been following me seemed to be getting closer! I frantically dodged the tombstones and ducked past the reaching branches. I ran until my feet bled but no matter how fast I ran *it* just seemed to get closer and closer ...

My legs could no longer keep up with my body. In a flash, without thinking, I turned round and as I did the world came crashing down. I had tripped, I was now lying face down with my head in the mud and *it* was breathing cold, icy air onto the back of my neck.

I turned round to surrender myself and as I looked up a bright light blinded me. Then surprisingly a warm, soft hand reached out to help me up. The light faded as it lit up the person's face; it was my friend. She had been following the whole time as she was worried about me walking through the graveyard on my own!

Jenny Reaney (14)
St Julie's High School, Woolton

The Night I Will Never Forget

It was a dark, cold Hallowe'en night. The wind banged against the doors of the villagers. The trees thrashed against each other as the wind seeped through their branches. Leaves and litter whirled round and round in circles and weaved in and out of trees.

After such a trivial argument with her friend, Rachel stormed out of the party, slamming the door as she left and was now beginning to regret it.

As she came to the end of the woods she began to hear very faint footsteps coming from behind her. She then came to a dark, gloomy graveyard. The wind whistled wildly as she carried on her long journey home. The footsteps began to get louder and clear so Rachel started to pick up her pace. *Why did I fall out with Chloe? Why did I storm out of the party on my own? This night will end in a disaster*, she thought to herself. She turned around to see who it was who was following her but no one was there. *Who is it?* she wondered.

By now Rachel was running as fast as her legs could carry her and the footsteps were louder than ever. She could hear someone breathing heavily behind her. *This is it*, she thought*, there is no point in carrying on*. She stopped. So did the footsteps. She could feel something warm and silky wrapping itself in-between her feet. She looked down to see her next-door neighbour's cat snuggled comfortably at her feet.

Sophie Nuttall (13)
St Julie's High School, Woolton

The Uninhabited House?

The rusty padlock covered in dust and cobwebs indicated the house was uninhabited.

As I touched the chain the rust and paint crumbled in my hands. My friend and I tried to push the door open, but we failed. All we could see was lanky trees with bats dangling from them and owls hooting in the night sky.

We walked around the house to see if we could enter through the back door. I prised the corroded hinges off using an old discarded garden spade.

Peter and I managed to pull the door ajar, immediately we were hit by an indescribable stench which made us baulk.

Although frightened we couldn't resist entering the dark, dingy house. My torch pierced the darkness, shedding light on a steep spiralling staircase. 'What are we waiting for?' I whispered.

We crept slowly up the creaking staircase, each step getting further and further into the unknown. My torch began to flicker, suddenly we heard scurrying across the bare floorboards, which seemed to echo in the darkness. I bashed it into the palm of my hand, it illuminated the landing to reveal four closed doors.

'Which one shall we open first?' Peter asked hesitantly. Our minds were soon made up when we heard scratching noises behind a closed door. I stretched my shaking arm out slowly and grabbed the door handle. Suddenly I saw something move. I shone my torch at the tall, dark figure, 'John!'

'You should have seen your faces,' exclaimed my twin John.

Katie Fitzpatrick (14)
St Julie's High School, Woolton

The Letter

It was London; 1914; a time of fear, anguish and despair; a time of war.

The war had been raging for six months now and every man and woman left behind had been left in shreds; torn apart, waiting to hear from the boys so far from home.

One of these once carefree people was Mary Weather-bout - a formerly beautiful young woman whose worries had left her face pale and with only a vestige of the great smile that once glittered upon it.

Mary's own letter was late so she put on her mask and stepped outside. Light from the moon filtered through the smoke clouds and, across the street, cast an eerie light upon the pale, skeletal body of a man, and the tonne of rubble he was sprawled across. However Mary did not rush over for fear he was a spy.

The man lifted his head. Mary stared and he let out a howl of pain. He was half-hidden by the smoke but Mary saw his shadow and felt his eyes burning at her through the yellow clouds.

He stretched out a hand and his fingers seemed to grapple at the thin air, reaching for her, she gasped ... and his hand fell still.

She could hold back no longer. She ran over.

And, it was then she found, to her horror, that the smoky tendrils coiled around him masked a naval uniform red with blood; a letter that belonged to her, and the face of her husband.

Jessica Cooke (14)
St Julie's High School, Woolton

The Walk In The Woods

Finally, it was the end of school, I couldn't wait to get home, it was my birthday, and my mum and dad were taking me and my friends out.

Walking home from school with Krya was so exciting, 'Be at mine for 6.30 and tell Jasmine, see you later.' I started walked home and I decided to take a short-cut through the woods.

As I reached half-way through the woods, I felt something touch my foot, I looked down but there was nothing there, I thought nothing of it so I carried on walking. I kept hearing noises, it was like a screeching sound, I was too scared to look back, I just carried on walking faster, but the noise was just following me, I was terrified.

I ran as fast as I could to the entrance, and eventually got there, now I was out in my street, I could still hear the noise. I felt safer so I decided to turn around, I thought I would have found a big scary man dressed in black, but instead there was a balloon attached to my foot by a string, I couldn't believe it! I couldn't wait to go to the pictures and tell my friends how daft I had been.

Lisa Ward (14)
St Julie's High School, Woolton

Under The Bed

I sat there, alone, chills running up my spine. I knew something was not quite right but still I stayed, motionless, just stiff under my duvet, hoping, praying this noise would go away. I didn't know what to do, a cold breeze swished over me, my skin tingled all over. I peeked over the duvet to find nothing, the window was wide open and the nets were flying up almost as if someone was hiding underneath them.

I felt helpless, too petrified to move, I pushed one leg out of my bed, it hovered there for a second or two, but then I heard the thumping again, I quickly pulled my leg back in and dived under the bed sheets. The mattress was starting to move, there was definitely something under there.

I finally plucked up the courage to get up and out of the bed. So I took a deep breath and ran over to the window, slammed it shut, pushed the nets back down and ran back to my bed, but as I ran I tripped over a skipping rope and fell flat onto my stomach looking straight underneath the bed. At first I could only see boxes but then suddenly something big jumped out. I screamed and closed my eyes then took a step back, only to find my little brother standing in front of me pointing and laughing. I'll remember next time to check where my brother is instead of getting so worked up!

Rebecca Cleghorn (14)
St Julie's High School, Woolton

Campsite Huckleberry Drive

Well there I was, walking onto the coach with Ella and Rachel, racing to the back seats. It was finally here, the trip we'd all been waiting for, but now was the long journey ahead.

We were there, standing in our dorm rooms, but now it was time for our traditional campfire. Miss Daniels went looking for wood. An hour had gone past, leaving the class shivering in the cold, wrapping their brown blankets from the dorms around them, no matter how rough they were. Ella, Rachel and I decided to go on a walk to find Miss Daniels.

We walked through the wild forest, through the wilderness. We were surrounded with trees and bushes and all there was in the distance was what seemed like a black sheet. The floor was a thick, misty fog surrounding our feet until they were invisible.

In the near distance were screams. Ella jumped in fear while Rachel screamed. I looked around in shock, the bushes started to move and a small black figure ran, exposing itself in the spaces.

We sprinted through the forest and thick, misty fog until our legs were numb and couldn't move.

There again was the rustling but this time it was from above and sounded as if it was coming from the tree.

Suddenly an object fell, it was Daniels, she was dead, with a thick tatty rope around her neck, her face soaked in blood and her eyes ripped out. The creature emerged from the bushes, this wasn't the end …!

Lauren Toller (13)
St Julie's High School, Woolton

The Crowd

It was a great move, a new lease of life my husband said. I opened the door of my new home, I felt a presence of people watching me, not a feeling I wanted as I stepped into 'my dream home'. But I shook off that feeling and began to unpack my things.

A few weeks later we had visitors round, I showed them round my home, I felt fine until I stepped back into the hall, again, that creepy presence. Suddenly I heard noises almost like a whisper. I made out some words, it said, 'Leave now!'

I said goodbye to my guests then went back into the hall, this time the whisper became more of a shout or a chant, 'Leave now! Leave now!' the chant raved on. I felt like the world was spinning, I had to get out of that house! As I ran to the door it was locked, surely I would have heard my husband come in. 'David, David are you home?' I hollered but he didn't reply. Out of nowhere all the doors closed in the house. I was left alone in this haunted house, I tried to open every door but something told me not to go upstairs.

I banged on the window to try and get any passers-by's attention, I had no luck. I turned back round and looked to the top of the stairs to see a sight so shocking I nearly died ... a crowd of dead bodies.

Helen Delaney (14)
St Julie's High School, Woolton

The 18th Century Agent

I stood there, my knees trembling, slowly getting weaker. My body sweating with heat even though I was as cold as ice inside. I walked towards the old wooden door. It seemed neglected and looked as if it hadn't been opened for centuries. There was a lock on the door and a key embedded in the dusty doormat below it. The lock creaked and clanked as I tried to open it. My hands blistered from the roughness of the lock. It finally opened and with one final push the door swung open.

Slowly I crept into the room, I shuddered, it was cold and creepy. It was dark; I looked around for a switch. I heard a quiet noise, almost like a whisper, getting louder as if it was coming towards me. I felt a sudden gust of wind brush past me. The hairs on the back of my neck stood up, a cold hand of fear touched the back of my shoulder. Suddenly I didn't feel alone anymore. I could hear footsteps, was it my imagination playing tricks on me or was there really something there?

I rummaged around in my pocket to find some sort of light. I grabbed my phone and flashed it around a couple of times, nothing. A quick glance and I saw her. She looked like an estate agent. Apparently she had been locked in the room while she was looking around. But how did she survive for so long I keep asking myself?

Amie Poole (13)
St Julie's High School, Woolton

Midnight Stalker

The clock struck twelve, and there was silence on Sunnybank Road. It was desolate, all was still and quiet. A small family of mice scurried out of the bushes to cross the road. The wind howled and the trees swayed. There was a shudder in the bushes, as a claw crunching in the gravel, grabbed one small mouse which trailed along behind the others. There was a squeal and a hiss, then silence once again. The rugged creature crept out into the moonlight.

A group of trouble-making teenagers, stumbled along the deserted road, laughter and chatter awoke people from their sleep. They returned to their homes, leaving the road abandoned once again, apart from one young girl who carried on towards the end of the road. The bushes shuddered as she passed them, she began to walk a little faster. She heard something strange, sort of like a whine. 'Who's there?' she asked. There was no reply. Her walk began to turn into a bit of a jog.

She felt something brush against her leg and she let out a shrill scream. Feeling her ankle snap she fell to the floor. Her tears trickled down her face, and she turned around to see …

'Mr Whiskers!' she said with a sigh of relief, 'I've been looking for you everywhere!'

A fat ginger cat purred, and rubbed against its owner.

The girl smiled, 'Come on let's go home.'

Jessica Mealey (13)
St Julie's High School, Woolton

Unwanted Visitors

Finally the day had come for Dave, Marie and family to move into the old Victorian house that had been empty for so long. They had spent months renovating, it was to be their dream house but what they didn't realise was that this house held a secret.

They had been in the house for a while, when Marie found herself, looking over her shoulder thinking somebody was there. She started to notice that, no matter which window she looked through, a black cat would be sitting there, watching her.

In one of the bedrooms where the secret was to unfold, when Marie entered, it felt cold and airy, she felt a presence and the cat would still be on the window sill.

One night when they were asleep, Marie suddenly woke up, objects were flying across the room, it felt windy. Marie wanted to scream but nothing came out, Dave and the baby slept through it all. She saw a figure of a man sitting by her bed watching her, with his hand stretched out to her. Marie held his hand and he took her into the room that she feared.

She felt that the ghost was trying to tell her something, but what?

Suddenly she felt herself opening the window to let the cat in, it stood by the ghost and they both disappeared.

That morning Marie found herself waking up in bed. She got up and went into the room, it was peaceful. Had it all been a dream?

Jessica Heaton (14)
St Julie's High School, Woolton

The Girl Next Door

Flat fourteen, first floor, just off Blake Close was owned by Amanda Buxton. Manda, as she was known to her friends, was a twenty-two year old nurse and worked in the local children's hospital. She had moved into the flat next door to her best friend Laura three months ago when it became available.

Manda had a challenging day at work with a young toddler dying and working a twelve-hour shift. Normally she would struggle to put the right key in the door through tiredness, but tonight she didn't feel tired in the slightest. She went into the living room to watch The Bill. The adverts came on, so Manda decided to make herself a cup of tea. She returned to find the television off and the remote nowhere to be seen. She put the cup down and went to look for it in the kitchen. She couldn't find it so switched it on at the television and went back to her cup of tea. That was when she froze. She dropped the now empty cup in horror. The tea had just disappeared into thin air!

Amanda now ran screaming to Laura's to find Laura almost crying with laughter.

'On you,' cried Laura.

'What are you laughing at? What do you mean?' Manda screamed.

'It was me you fool!' laughed Laura, 'there is a cupboard leading to your flat from mine.'

Amanda joined in the laughter with Laura at how stupid she had been.

Rachel Higgins (14)
St Julie's High School, Woolton

Behind Closed Doors

Number 97 Hysteria Drive sat upon an overgrown garden in the corner of the road. The odd one out compared to the rest of the houses in Hysteria Drive, the other houses had perfectly manicured gardens, neatly co-ordinated curtains and perfect families who lived in them. On the other hand, number 97 had remained derelict and dishevelled for the past nine years.

Nine years ago today, the Morgan family mysteriously disappeared and number 97 fell silent. Four days later the Morgan family were found gruesomely murdered in their home.

There I was, walking through that very house myself. The ragged curtains that limply hung from the windows blocked the orange glow from the street lamps outside. I came across an old oak door, I was curious as to what was behind it. My hand fell upon the rusty door handle. I slowly turned it and gently opened the door. An unexpected gush of cold air blew in my face and a sudden shiver travelled down my spine.

I was in a drawing room. All the other rooms in the house had been vandalised except the room I was standing in. It hadn't been touched in nine years. The oak door suddenly slammed shut! I ran towards it and tried to pull it open. As much as I tried it wouldn't move. I started to panic.

Something was breathing down the back of my neck. I turned around, let out a scream and ...

I was never seen by my family again ...

Holly Gates (14)
St Julie's High School, Woolton

A Day In The Life Of A Tiger In Captivity

Have you ever wondered what it would be like to be deprived of everything you ever knew?

If you had witnessed your mother being mercilessly slaughtered, your father slain for human greed?

Then wonder no more, listen to my story.

Awaking from my slumber, the long line of curious faces peered through the steel bars of my musty cage. A short, plump lady, with shocking auburn hair, began poking me, attempting to catch my tail. I longed for the jungle, to live life in the paradise I once called home. My beautiful home was destroyed that fateful day, my parents shot down like trees being felled. If only I could regain my regal power and, once again, roam the jungle free, as king, but I knew my destiny belonged in this tiny cage.

I heard the sinister laugh of the circus owner. The delicious aroma of candyfloss filled my nostrils and the faint sound of a carousel echoed in my ear. I despised that sound. That was the sound I heard the day my mother was killed.

'Little cub, how's your mother?' cackled the keeper. 'My wife wears her every day! Very complimentary is tiger skin!'

He led me out.

I observed the familiar crowd and the hoop glowing with burning flames. I knew exactly what to do. I had done it a million times before. Three foot would clear the hoop safely. I smiled secretly, knowing that in one jump this nightmare would be over. I deliberately jumped low.

Stephanie Shannon (13)
St Julie's High School, Woolton

All Alone

After months of concealing my bump from everyone I knew the moment I had dreaded had arrived. As the pains grew stronger I rushed to my cramped room, clenching my stomach.

I found it increasingly difficult not to scream. If my social worker Karen heard me she would enter my room in a flash.

Hours passed and suddenly I had a screaming baby lying helplessly beside me. I held her in my arms, how I wished Mark was here with me. It was my fault he was transported to another care home. I confided in Karen how much I loved him. She betrayed me and told Mrs Winston, he was then taken away.

Panicking I clasped my hand over the baby's mouth desperately trying to make her quiet. Hurriedly I seized a towel and carefully wrapped her up.

I crept quietly down the stairs and out of the door. I wiped the streaming tears from my eyes. I gently caressed her cheek and kissed her delicate forehead.

I found it hard to prise the baby from my firm grip but knew it was the only chance she would have of not being brought up in a grubby children's home. I prayed someone would find and raise her as their own.

Hurriedly I placed her in a rose bush in the park.

'Sleep tight angel,' I whispered softly. I kissed her ... then ran as fast as I could. I left her howling in the cold, dark, dirty park ... all alone.

Kate Rimmer (13)
St Julie's High School, Woolton

Home Alone

They've left me alone again. Sitting in my basket, I need to go outside, stretch my legs. But they just don't understand. Maybe it's something I did. Maybe I wasn't loyal enough; maybe my barking drove them insane.

My food bowl is running low and my water disappeared days ago. On my last count I had been alone for five days. My golden fur is falling and my stomach is shrinking. I can barely stand up to walk.

I've been barking for hours, but nobody comes. I think my owner has truly left me this time. He's never been away this long. My throat is hoarse from barking but nobody listens to dogs do they, do they? We're here to look cute and to entertain our owners.

I don't think I'm going to survive much longer. My mouth is really dry, my bark has no sound, I can barely whine.

I can hear someone banging on the door. Maybe it's my owner. I hope it is, I need a drink. I don't think I can go on that much longer.

'Open up, we've had reports of animal cruelty.'

That's not my owner's voice! That's a woman! Maybe she'll feed me.

Bang! The door fell off the wall, a young woman has scooped me up and wrapped me in a blanket, she holds me close. She reads my name tag and says, 'Don't worry Louie we'll take you somewhere safe.'

She places me carefully in the back of the van and takes me to a better life.

Becky Evans (13)
St Julie's High School, Woolton

A Day In The Life Of A Child Soldier

The heavy wind blows rain upon my back. Tears sting my eyes and they roll down my cheeks. He yells abuse at me and expresses his anger through the savage way he strikes me with his whip. I expect to be beaten, because at six years of age I'm weak and my work is not up to standard.

I remember the day I was taken. My father lay in a pool of blood, my mother wept by his side. I was hurried away, threatened at gunpoint, I heard a gunshot behind me, *goodbye Mummy*, I told myself. I was taken prisoner and forced to work.

Now my life has totally changed. I am woken by a vicious man roaring in my face as droplets of saliva sprayed me. I feel faint with the heat and lack of food and water. I often collapse. My heart aches and yearns for love. Nobody will love me as what I have done is terrible, so terrible my actions torture me in my dreams.

I am forced to murder people. I cannot bear it. I was given a gun as soon as I came to this camp. When I am face to face with a victim I clench my clammy fists, squeeze my eyes shut and ... *bang!* They are dead. As quickly as that. Just like my beloved parents. Just as cruel, hurtful and sickening as my parents' murder. Someday I will be reunited with them. My heart mended by everlasting love.

Amanda Niker (12)
St Julie's High School, Woolton

A Day In The Life Of A Child Soldier

Ever since I can remember I have been a fighter, but there is one day that will stick in my mind forever.

My best friend and I were on patrol duty. As we loaded our rifles and put on our fatigues, I had a feeling something would happen.

Walking through the long grass, we heard a deafening boom. Landmines. We changed our course and headed west, where more danger awaited.

We surrounded the enemy, many of them my age, but a large number were grown men. All with a look of hatred in their eyes.

We glanced at each other. We knew the time had come for us to prove ourselves in the eyes of our sergeant major. Clutching our rifles, we shouted a warning then watched as many of the children fled.

'They will be punished later,' one of the large men who led them muttered under his breath.

We held our ground. None of us moved. Silence. All around. No escape.

Suddenly, and without warning, the large man who spoke before fired a shot. Quickly, I dived to the floor as we had been instructed. My friend, Marcus seemed paralysed with fear. His legs turned to lead. His face to stone. Despite my warnings, he was hit.

One shot to the heart and he fell. I watched as the tears and blood flowed. I watched his last breath. I watched my best friend die. He was ten years old.

Nancy Clarke (13)
St Julie's High School, Woolton

A Day In The Life Of A Footballer

So here I am, hot, tired and sweaty. Running up and down the pitch, going in for tackles, hoping to score a goal. My heart pounding every time the ball is on target with the goal, knowing that it might go in. Telling my co-workers to pass me the ball every time I am free, reminding myself why we need to score a goal. As I listen to the excited, devoted fans cheer us on with their songs and clapping I feel honoured to be here.

No! Now the whistle has been blown my heart sinks, the game has finished, we have lost to a three-two defeat! My chance of scoring has gone. All the hard work in that game has come to nothing, it was a waste of time. Feeling weak I walk across the pitch exhausted, clapping my hands to show the fans were great and so were the players even if we didn't win.

In the changing rooms there is silence, thinking to myself I realise we played well, fantastic even. We may not have won the Carling Cup but so what! We're going to win the Champions League - they won't.

Georgia Kemble (13)
St Julie's High School, Woolton

The Beginning

I am frightened. This darkness that I am used to now seems scary. The darkness is engulfing me, closing in on me. I don't feel any pain yet, just fear. Those comforting noises which once lulled me to sleep now seem far away. Replaced by new sounds, unfamiliar sounds.

I remember a time before this. I was comfortable, relaxed and sleepy. Just thinking about how I wanted to stay here forever. It is hard to believe that just a few hours ago I was peaceful yet now I feel as though my death is near.

Am I dying? Is this what death is really like? I always assumed that it would be graceful and painfree, but this is starting to hurt. The space that I am confined to is gradually becoming smaller.

I feel great sorrow for those who have died as they must have felt this terrible pain.

When people pass away innocent and sinless, aren't they meant to see a light? A light which guides them in the right direction?

I can see the light now, far in the distance. Should I go towards it? If I do will that be the end? What will be left of me?

Yes I will go towards this mysterious light, I need to break free from this trap, this pain.

Slowly I am getting closer, the light getting brighter, the new noise growing louder.

I am free! No pain! The light is now so bright I fear to open my eyes and look at my surroundings.

There is a high pitched noise. It's coming from me! Hang on ... what am I wrapped in? It's warm yet irritating ... it's so ...

'Congratulations, it's a baby girl!'

Hannah Dutton (14)
St Julie's High School, Woolton

A Day In The Life Of A Rat

A huge thud woke me once more from my disturbed sleep. I knew it was time to start running for my life. *Thump, thump!* Then something caught my tail. I squirmed and wriggled, trying to get away. Then I realised what it was that had picked me up with its small, sticky hands. A child. It looked at me blankly, then shook me up and down as if I was a ketchup bottle.

I woke up feeling so sick and dizzy, then I saw a huge, turquoise-looking eye staring right at my black ones. I pounced back startled, as it moved closer. A stubby finger flicked at me. It was then when I realised, the finger didn't reach me, it seemed to stop a few centimetres before. I looked up, down and everywhere around me, moved around and it hit me. I was stuck inside a stuffy glass jar.

The young boy stumbled and fell, as he did this he hit the table and slammed the jar. It was my exit. I ran and ran until I got to the end of the table. I was out of breath and didn't know where to go.

Slam! I was back in the jar again.

Raechel Clarke (13)
St Julie's High School, Woolton

A Day In The Life Of A Homeless Child

I looked up hopefully as I heard footsteps from around the corner. A young woman with a pram and lots of shopping bags appeared.

'Any change please?' I asked. She walked past as though I wasn't even there but her baby stared and pointed. I felt tears rising in the back of my eyes. It was always the same; people treated me as though I didn't exist but they didn't realise that I had feelings too, and it hurt me when they ignored me or pointed and laughed.

I leaned back and sat against the doorway, I looked around at my home: the plastic bags, the thin sheet I used to keep warm and the cold, stone steps I sat and slept on.

A brand new Mercedes drove past, sitting inside was a family of four, Mum, Dad, big brother and little sister. I turned away, they all looked so happy, it made me feel so sad. But losing Mum and Dad and my younger brother John had made me grow up very quickly, even though I was only 12 I felt a lot older.

An elderly couple were walking towards me. As they came nearer I asked again, 'Any change please?'

The woman looked at me kindly and stopped. She opened her bag and pulled a pound coin out of her purse and placed it next to me. She smiled, linked her husband's arm and walked away.

Tomorrow that will buy me dinner, I thought as I huddled under the thin sheet for an uncomfortable night's sleep.

Hannah Murphy (14)
St Julie's High School, Woolton

What Will Happen Next?

A single bead of cold sweat trickled down my face, my pounding heart bursting out of my chest. My feet stumbled over a loose flagstone and I lost a shoe, but I didn't care. I just kept running and running, not daring to turn around. I could hear them gaining on me, laughing and shouting. I turned sharply into a side street to try and escape. Suddenly I realised it was a dead end. As I whipped around I saw them blocking my only exit. There was no way out. I was trapped ...

I've always known I would never be accepted. Somehow I knew they had some sort of grudge against me even though I'd never met them before. They would say things like, 'You owe me!' and 'I'll never forget what you've done!' and no matter how much I tried to find out, they would never tell me.

They would do the usual things - push and shove me, take my money, but today there was something different. They were being nice to me and foolishly I thought they were genuine. They asked me to go to the shop with them and I agreed. I'd rather try to be friends with them than be on the receiving end of their torment.

However, as I got out my money to pay, they scowled at me and threw me looks as sharp as knives.

'We don't pay!' they hissed, and for some reason, I don't know why, I ran.

So that's why I'm here now, scared for my life, not knowing what will happen next.

Katherine Gilroy (13)
St Julie's High School, Woolton

A Day In The Life Of An Evacuee In The Second World War

I missed her. I really missed her. How I longed to be close to her, talk to her, see her. I cried when I awoke from my sweet dream. The two of us together playing in the park, just as it used to be, both of us together.

I was startled as Mrs Williams shouted upstairs, 'Hurry up, go out for your morning walk.'

So off I went, alone. I walked miles and miles from what was now my home. I didn't see a single child to play with, just luscious green grass and tall towering trees. I hated this time, all I could think of was her.

I walked home for my lunch, poached egg on toast, her favourite. She was constantly on my mind.

In the afternoon I walked to the nearest village to buy all we could with the ration book: bacon, eggs, bread, milk. I then returned to Mrs William's house. How I wished I was home once more, cuddled up to her, I missed her, I wanted to go home.

I gloomily went upstairs into my room. It was cold, dark, not homely at all as I sat alone. I wanted her to hold me, not let me go.

After dinner, up I went. I sat on my bed, I closed my eyes. I was on the sofa, warm in her embrace, she wouldn't let go, we had to stay together.

All I wanted was to be there, home in my house in London, home with my mum.

Caroline Walsh (13)
St Julie's High School, Woolton

Joy Riding

I couldn't feel anything, other than a numb, buzzing sensation all over my body. My mouth was dry, and I couldn't open my eyes. Suddenly I heard a trembling voice, 'How did this happen? Why? What did she do to deserve this?'

The gentle sobbing voice belonged to my mother. I could have told her, I kept having tormented flashbacks. The window winding down, 'You can trust me,' those words playing over and over again, a man's voice broke my thoughts.

'The chances of her waking up are very slim. The machine is keeping her alive, you must consider switching the machine off.'

My mother cried out. I couldn't understand what was happening, I was awake, wasn't I?

'Mum,' I called, 'I'm here, I'm okay.'

'Is she in pain?'

'Dad!' I shouted, why were they ignoring me?

'No, she's in a coma, she cannot feel anything.'

The flashbacks returned, a red car, his trustworthy eyes luring me in. I knew it was wrong, but everybody was watching me. I climbed in. Why did I do it?

'I'm not in a coma! Why won't you listen? Turn the machine off, I will still be here!'

The van coming towards us, we were travelling at unbelievable speed, then ... nothing. Just darkness. No pain at all.

'It's the kindest thing to do, but it is your decision.'

'Mum, turn it off. I don't need it. I'm fine.'

'Okay, switch the machine off. She doesn't deserve to suffer anymore.'

I gasped as my remaining breath was pulled out of me, it was over.

Caroline Doherty (14)
St Julie's High School, Woolton

Escaped Chimps Cause Chaos

Today there has been a major search for a group of escaped chimps who have been causing chaos in the city of Chester.

These cheeky chimps escaped from the famous Chester Zoo at midnight last night.

Since then this group of vandals have been running riot and causing mayhem in the local village.

They have been stealing clothes and washing lines in many back gardens, and have been playing 'dressing up' a secret source told us yesterday.

'I saw a gang of what I thought were drunken youths, running round the street in old ladies dresses and hats.

They are also thought to have been the cause of the power cut, after vandalising aerials and telegraph poles.

Police officers are now on the look out for this threatening gang.

Many elderly citizens are in fear of these monkeys and will not leave the house until they are caught.

A spokesperson from Chester Zoo has assured us that the chimps are not lethal, but when provoked they will attack in self-defence.

A helpline has been set up for the public so they can phone in and give information to help capture the escapees.

Chester Zoo have placed a reward of £1000 to whoever captures these chimps and brings them back safely.
Until then we can only live in fear and hope that they are caught soon.

Katie Guy (13)
St Julie's High School, Woolton

A Day In The Life of A Designer

I couldn't believe it - me a designer - me, my name on everyone's bags, clothes and even shops.

This morning I woke up, as usual, to an ordinary day. I went to work; my job was in an office, helping design and encourage new merchandise like Dior to become multi-millionaires. If we were lucky, which I was, you could become a famous designer yourself.

I received the news that business was booming for me because of my most recent design of bags and they were selling quickly. Gratefully with my heart pounding, my boss handed over a cheque for guess what ...? A million pounds! I grabbed it shakily. He said, 'You've worked hard for this, now you can be what you've always wanted - rich!'

That all happened over a fortnight ago, now I'm sitting in my penthouse, sipping some champagne elegantly and living the life of luxury.

The first thing I bought was two cars, a Lexus and a limousine. The Lexus is just for the usual day and the limousine is for night-time.

Some of my usual daytime activities involve leisurely things such as ice skating, swimming and last but definitely not least, shopping! I call it retail therapy.

A regular night-time for me is eating out of 'Mirantos'. I'm that restaurant's most loyal customer. After that I dance the night away at Atlantic City, the most popular club.

I hope you don't think this all sounds shallow as I have given some money to charity.

Hannah Jones (13)
St Julie's High School, Woolton

A Day In The Life Of A Fireman

Briiinngg! the bell went once again. I jumped up and ran down to the fire engine, frantically trying to pull on my uniform. I jumped into the engine and we drove into the blackness of the night, the lights of the siren the only thing to guide us, the sound echoing down the streets.

We turned down the right road and we immediately saw the house we were meant to be at. The house looked like a huge bonfire: red, yellow, orange and pink filled the street. All the neighbours were out, some crying out of terror for the people trapped inside waiting for the rescuers, us. The air was filled with ash and smelt musty.

I pushed my way to the front; my uniform weighing me down. I had hold of the hose and could feel my colleagues behind me. I pushed open the door and was blinded momentarily from the smoke that bellowed from the door. The heat hit me like a slap in the face as I took my first step. I knew someone was in the house that I needed to rescue. I pulled on the trigger of the hose and a jet of cool liquid blanketed the flames. I passed the hose to the person next to me. I ran up the stairs each step seeming higher as I got nearer the top. The smoke engulfing my lungs, filling them up. I heard a scream and sped up. The scream stopped.

Was I too late?

Stephanie McKeown (13)
St Julie's High School, Woolton

A Day In The Life Of A Prisoner

Every morning I wake up to the sound of wardens voices screaming, 'Get up!' to wake the prisoners. Today, my cellmate, a serial killer, is shouting through the cell bars that he's innocent. His victims think otherwise. But me, I am innocent. I shouldn't be in here.

At about 10.00 we have to be ready to work. I clean the toilets while my cellmate is watched as he picks up rubbish and cleans the bins.

After an hour of working, we have something to eat, if we've done a good job. Although the food is absolutely vile, it is one of three meals we get a day and so I have to eat it to stop myself from dying of starvation.

It's so horrible; I get threatened every day for being a wimp. I can only take every day as it comes. After we've eaten we have an hour to ourselves when we can do what we like.

At 6 o'clock, it's visiting time, all my friends get good news from their wives or mothers, while I sit there in my cell waiting and wishing that today the warden would come and tell me my wife or brother was here. But week after week I sit here just looking at photographs of them.

When we've had tea at 7 o'clock, I go to bed, dreaming of the day I can be released from this hellhole.

Kate O'Hara (13)
St Julie's High School, Woolton

A Day In The Life Of a Soldier

It was the crack of dawn, I was awoken with an almighty bang and jumped up in shock. The ground shook as though there was an earthquake and there was a sequence of explosions.

I quickly climbed out of the trench and the sight I saw sickened me. Someone had trodden on a landmine that set off a series of explosions. I rushed out as quickly as I could, to see if there were any survivors among the pile of bodies. All I could think of was that they were my friends out there. I found two survivors out of thirty bodies. I made it back to the trench with one over each shoulder, they were barely alive but still breathing. The doctor took over from there.

After the landmines went off there was never a moment of silence with constant gunfire and bombs. Suddenly there was a boom as a plane was shot down; unfortunately it was one of ours. I couldn't see or breathe for smoke, it was choking. I spent all day bringing back bodies.

It had been the worst day so far, I was really missing my family. I would take out a photo of them every night before I went to sleep in case I did not make the next day.

I was exhausted but relieved to have survived another day, when I felt the explosion. I took my last every gasp and closed my eyes. I knew I had to go.

Eleanore Craig (13)
St Julie's High School, Woolton

A Day In The Life Of An Orphan

I woke up this morning to the sound of rain hitting the ground surrounding me. I was used to getting wet but not because I had a refreshing shower every day but because I live outside. I'm an orphan.

I have nobody, every day is the same. I walk up and down the streets searching for money or food. It's a hard life.

Today however is different. After I collected my belongings together, (little of which there actually is) I began to walk the streets. After about two hours I had to have a rest so I sat down for a while.

Suddenly I heard the sound of a small girl crying. I followed the sound to a small alley where I saw her alone by a wall. I approached her and asked her what was wrong. She replied, 'I'm lost, I can't find my mummy.' She showed me where she had last seen her mum and together we found her.

The little girl's mum was so ecstatic that I was asked back to her house. The lady's house was like nothing I had ever seen before. The rooms were all decorated in beautiful colours with real wood furniture. To them it was nothing but for me it was the world. I ate a brilliant feast with them and watched television. Then we went to bed.

So here I am in a bed. God what difference a day can make.

Katy Jones (13)
St Julie's High School, Woolton

The Sign

Have you ever witnessed that experience where you get a cold, eerie shiver down your back, but don't know why?

Have you ever considered that it actually might happen because of the paranormal?

Well, that happened to me. It occurred last Hallowe'en, when I had a few friends around to stay. One of my friends had brought their old Ouija board, but none of us thought that it was going to be that frightening ... but we were very wrong ...

We tried it out, and all of a sudden, the room started to tremble. As my porcelain dolls smashed as they fell off the shelf, my friends and I screamed and panicked with fear, all edging away from the Ouija board, when a burst of mist appeared from beyond, and a strangely familiar face appeared, and howled, 'Beware of the sign ...' chanting it in a sinister way. Suddenly a strange sign appeared in the mirror, and then disappeared into darkness.

I suddenly jolted up, feeling afraid and nervous, it was only a nightmare ... but as I got out of bed to brush my teeth, I noticed something very familiar in my mirror. It was the sign ... and that was when I experienced that cold, eerie shiver down my back.

Bernadette Clarke (13)
St Julie's High School, Woolton

A Day In The Life Of A Farm Pig

His legs strained, his face distressed, carrying yet again an overflowed barrel of delicious food.

He's been rather generous lately, the farmer, forever supplying us with crates of surprises. Maybe he struck gold or divorced that wicked witch of a wife! I mean, I don't want to sound ungrateful, but I am beginning to feel sick of eating so much, as though someone has slipped a spare tyre around my waist.

Another rumour which has aroused excitement around the farm is that pigs are being sent away on splendid holidays! Tranquil surroundings, mud lakes, everything a pig could hope for. Only, being such a caring and intelligent pig, I have noticed the absence of previous holiday travellers who don't seem to ever return. They must have unfortunately lost their way home or chosen not to return as they were having so much fun!

Anyway, moving away from the subject, here comes the poor farmer again, however he is free from any heavy weight, only a small rope.

'Come on little piggy,' he whispered in my ear. I have always known I was special and a credit to own but why was he taking me away? He quickly wrapped me, very gently in a red stained rope, and it seemed we were heading for the barn - heaven knows why! Once we were inside, he suddenly placed me onto a large, worn cardboard box. At this moment, it struck me why all the above things were happening!

The room was dark, filled with a musty smell. Inside all that could be seen was the glint of sharp objects, one of which occupied the farmer's shaking hands. I realised this was my end.

Melissa Longworth (14)
St Julie's High School, Woolton

A Day In The Life Of A Newborn Baby

It's so bright and noisy out here, I miss the comfort and warmth of my watery bed. I feel like a stranger, the same two familiar faces keep kissing and hugging me. Who are they? I heard a woman who seems to be aiming to torture me, say that one was called Mum and another Dad. What strange names, mind you not as strange as the name people say as they talk to me, 'Emma', I am so confused, how am I supposed to remember all of this?

Another thing that is bugging me is when I try to tell these people that I'm hungry they just seem to want to shut me up by forcing a soft, rubbery, strange looking tube filled with a white liquid into my mouth. Though the liquid doesn't taste that bad it is quite sweet and is very wholesome and filling, my stomach may burst at any moment, people keep saying I'm a podge, wonder what they mean?

That annoying woman is back again, her icy-cold fingers send shivers up my spine, she lays me uncomfortably on a silver, shiny looking dish, poking and prodding from my head to my toes, she always seems to disturb me when my eyes are drifting off to their slumber!

More strangers have arrived, again passing me round like a parcel, one is 'Auntie', another 'Grandad', and another nearly as small as me is 'Cousin Tom'. As if the sloppy kisses weren't enough, a black object keeps making a big flash that hurts my eyes as everyone tries to cuddle in close. How will I ever get used to this!

Aimi Hodgson (14)
St Julie's High School, Woolton

Guilty

As I looked around I couldn't believe where I was, sat in a hospital next to my dad, all I could hear was his heart machine, *beeeeep!* I couldn't believe I had been so stupid. This morning I had a family, now my parents are dead. I'm so glad Mark's with me, I know it's my fault I'm here, if I hadn't of snuck out, my parents wouldn't have come looking for me and crashed the car.

My parents are dead and all I can do is cry, the tears are endless. My parents never noticed me before so what difference will it make now. I've snuck out every night for months, and they haven't even noticed, so why did they come looking tonight.

My life is over, I can't believe that everyone blames me, I know it was my fault, but if my parents had taken an interest in my life, I would have been happier but they didn't, they just ignored me.

I know it sounds stupid, but I can't go into care, my social worker said that I would have to move away, because my family thinks I'm being badly influenced. What do they know, I'm a good kid. Mark's just given me some pills, to help me relax. I know what they are, and I don't know what I'm doing, I always refused before. Maybe I shouldn't have taken them, I feel like I'm about to collapse, I can't see properly. My head's throbbing, I can't remember anything, I feel like I'm about to fall asleep.

Elizabeth Devine (13)
St Julie's High School, Woolton

A Day In The Life Of An Unwanted Baby

I woke to the loud cries of my so-called mummy screaming for help. The floor shuddered, my cot shook. The loud hollow cries stopped abruptly, the door slammed. This was a normal day in my life.

Curling up with my blanket was the only thing that gave me comfort. I started to doze, dreaming of what life could have been like if Mummy and Daddy really loved me.

Shaking fiercely, I opened my eyes to find Mummy standing over my cot. She didn't look at me with those warm eyes anymore. Her face very pale, she had those funny marks, which when I touched she turned away. Lifting me up, I could tell Mummy was weak. She held me close to her chest. Her heart beating extremely quick.

Having fed me my lunch, I was left on my own to play in my pen. Glancing over to Mummy every odd time I noticed her face swelling, the marks getting worse. When Mummy was on the phone, she began crying, the tears running slowly down her harmed face. I did not know what was happening, all I knew was that Mummy was hurting.

Hours passed, still I remained in my pen. Having played with all my toys, I lay quietly on the cold floor waiting for Mummy to come and get me. It was hard to know how long I would be left here.

Emerging from the kitchen, Mummy looked powerless, frail, old, as if she had no strength.

Carrying me close to her heart, Mummy tucked me into my cot. Falling asleep I thought how my day had been. Mummy and Daddy showing me no love, it made me feel unwanted. Was I worth nothing to them?

Sian Lundy (14)
St Julie's High School, Woolton

Terror Tower Nightmare

Everybody has heard the tale of the haunted theme park, the ghoul-filled ghost train and roller coasters that never end, but I was sure, positive, that nothing was going wrong that day. So I put these thoughts to the back of mind and entered 'Wallies Crazy Town'.

A few hours later and several hundred roller coaster rides later, I was certain all the rides had been ridden (perhaps several times over) by myself and John, so we settled on a grass verge for a hot-dog.

The sun was bold and beaming, a perfect day. I turned to John, he had now turned green, he didn't feel too comfortable with the 'Twizzle Torture'. 'Can we go now?' he pleaded.

'Yeah, guess so ... we've tried all the rides,' I answered.

Suddenly I spotted, hidden behind the worn away candyfloss machine, a sign, 'Terror Tower'.

John saw me gaze in awe at the sign and was quick to distract me. 'No, no, it's abandoned, no one's there, let's just go.'

But he couldn't stop me, my determination to go on every single ride shone through and a minute later we were ready to ride the 'Terror Tower'.

Chuttering along in the ancient cart, my mind was somewhere else, this truly was a boring ride, no wonder it was closed! As these thoughts passed my mind the cart swerved to a halt, paused, then began racing backwards. So fast I couldn't see. Ghosts, ghouls, shrieks of laughter followed me. We halted, then jerked forwards, John's whimpering forced me to open my eyes. Confused I searched for people, no one, we stood, frozen, alone in total darkness. I realised the 'Terror Tower' was boring no more.

Siân Falshaw (14)
St Julie's High School, Woolton

A Day In The Life Of Mighty Joe Young

It only took a few seconds and suddenly I was all alone. Me and four black walls and two strangers in the front. I knew I had to get away from these men. The men who had tormented me all my life. The men who killed Jill's mum and mine. I realised if I didn't do anything I would be left with no one. Jill was the only person who didn't harm me.

I stood up and the thought of what the men had done to me, made me cause the vehicle to crash. Straight away I broke out of the dark box and lights stared me in the face. I thought it was Jill signalling to me but as I approached it, it was just rays of light coming from something supposedly called a fair.

I turned around and all I could see was the hunter. Tears ran down from my eyes, as Jill wasn't in my sight. Anger came to me so quickly that I knocked over the bundle of lights and suddenly flames went up just beneath my nose.

The happiness of children turned into cries as the flames grew bigger. The fair soon cleared and there was no one except smoke and myself until I heard a loud cry. I looked around and noticed a young boy screaming, *'Help!'*

I ran over straight away and climbed to the top of this huge wheel. The flames grew higher and the wheel started to tilt. My hopes of saving the boy fell until I noticed Jill in the distance. I decided to jump and as the tears dried from under my eyes, my whole world went blank.

Lindsey Dixon (13)
St Julie's High School, Woolton

A Day In The Life Of A Lab Animal

It's a hard life, this, I mean all I've done is been born a guinea pig and somehow I'm being poked and prodded every second of the day! My other two brothers Berty and Bill, they're fine, in a big warm house with loving owners caring for them. But me, Betty, I get taken away by some 'scientists' and get products tested on me all day. I was always the unlucky one in the family.

Last week was pretty awful, they decided to try anti-wrinkle cream on me. At first I was over the moon because I thought to myself at least it'll get rid of my crows feet, but it didn't even work! The only thing that did happen is that my body began to feel like it was on fire, burning, and my fur began to feel very sticky and uncomfortable. Even so I still think they're going to sell it!

Yesterday was pretty horrific; I had hair straighteners tested on me. However they put them too near my skin and gave me an electric shock! I had shivers down my spine, I did! And I've got a big burn on my back and it's itching me like mad!

Today was just the tip of the iceberg! Some kind of medical needles were tested on me. At first it was just a prick, but then it began to throb and now the whole left side of my body is numb.

They just don't understand how much it hurts!

Phoebe Donnelly (13)
St Julie's High School, Woolton

A Day In The Life Of A Remote Control

I woke up this morning feeling very stiff. I was lying on a glass shelf, surrounded by grey plastic. I had a big hexagonal box staring down at me, looking like it was about to cave in and squash me, it was only held up by three 'legs' and they were holding at least one glass shelf and maybe even others.

Then I heard an alarm, and a banging of feet coming down the stairs, the door swung open and two little boys came rushing in.

Oh no! I thought.

Both of them came running over and picked me up.

This is going to hurt!

I could feel the two ends of me getting pulled in different directions.

Crash!

They had dropped me on the floor, this hurt even more than the pulling.

Thankfully, this time only one of the little boys picked me up, but I was still in pain from the drop.

All of a sudden I felt a tickle, they were changing the channel.

Ooh, not again.

Luckily, after a few minutes my batteries ran out. They realised, so stopped tickling me. Then I remembered ...

Ouch!

I was dropped again.

Another man came in and placed me back on the shelf while chasing the boys out. At this I fell asleep, but was woken a couple of hours later. I felt myself getting opened up; they must have changed the batteries because then the tickling and dropping started again.

I'm glad this only lasted one day!

Laura Woodward (14)
St Julie's High School, Woolton

A Day In The Life Of Channel Williams

Sitting on her cold stair step scared, and trying her hardest to forget the trauma and the pain that was happening in the house, Channel Williams sat alone wondering what would be her father's next move.

She walked the corridors of the house silently trying not to make the slightest sound, trying not to disturb her father in case she upset him. This would be a foolish mistake to make as she knew the outcome would be bad. She had heard the screams from the step she sat upon every night. Screams from her mother then, abusive language from her so-called father. Every night she prayed to get out and dreamt of what it would be like to be a different girl in a different family, however she didn't want to leave her mother with this 'man'.

If Channel had known that day would be her last she would have done things differently.

This day was different to the rest. Usually her father never touched her but that day he raised his hand. Channel had never felt so much pain, she could feel the blood pouring from her nose, the swelling of her lip, the bruising on her ribs. She could hear her mother's cries, 'Leave her alone, please, oh Jim.' He didn't stop, harder and harder he hit her, his face emotionless staring into her eyes, watching her face become battered and bruised. Channel became motionless and became numb, she just froze, she didn't try and defend herself, she just lay there staring at her mother who was standing in the bedroom doorway cowering. Channel lay thinking, why didn't I tell someone? Why didn't I try and stop him? Why did it turn out like this? Why did my father turn on us? Was it me? Was I a bad daughter? Then she realised it wasn't her fault her father turned on her family, it was his fault. He was the reason her childhood was a disaster, not her, he was the problem, no one else. Suddenly her father stopped, he looked at her and her mother once again and walked down the staircase and left.

Her mother ran to Channel's side, crying and holding her tight, trying to comfort her. As Channel looked down she saw blood on her mother's hand and she hoped it wasn't her own. Then her mum stood up and walked into the bathroom, Channel thought she was going to wash the blood off her hands but she came back into the room with a bottle in her hand and she took one sip and collapsed on the floor.

With her last breath she said, 'You're going to a better place than here, have no fear, be a brave girl and God will look after you. I will see you there soon. I fear, this is the only way it can end. Please be strong for both of us and we'll look down on your little brother from up there. It won't be long so tell the angels to wait for me.'

Channel felt a pain greater than what she felt when her dad hit her, the feeling that knowing her dad had won and now she and her mother would leave the world being just another victim not a survivor, just another victim of her father's fist.

Channel's heartbeat became weaker and weaker, she gasped for breath, she whispered to her mother, 'I love you, please don't leave, come quick and be by my side.' Her heart stopped, her eyes gently closed. That was her last breath in the last day of her short-lived life which was cruelly taken away from her.

Gemma Blackburn (13)
St Julie's High School, Woolton

A Day In The Life Of A Cat

I woke up at around half-past nine, but life's tough! I thought I was a bit hungry, so I let out a little miaow and my bowl was filled, instantly! Well, it's not my fault they like me!

I didn't like my food, so I decided to go outside, ooh, there's a nice sunny spot! That cheeky cat sprawled out on the garden bench and left nowhere for anybody to sit!

I'm bored now, I'll go inside.

'Get off my kitchen table, you naughty cat!'

Uh oh, time to put on my cute and innocent face.

What can I say? It works every time, she always says, 'Ahh, my precious little baby!' It's pathetic! I want to go outside now ... *Miaow, miaow!* The door was opened for me! Mmmm ... a bird. Slowly, slowly and ... *pounce!* Oh, it got away! Time to go in now; I'm getting bored. Quarter to two in the morning now would be the time to have a mad hour!

Leap! Spring! Bounce! Run!

'Shh! Stupid cat!'

Ooh, a pair of feet hanging out of the bed, I just can't resist ... *pounce!*

'Owwww!'

What are you looking at me for? I mean, I am a cat!

Katie Maysmor (13)
St Julie's High School, Woolton

One Life For Another

What have I done? I stare at the cold, black monster in my hand; I look at the blood spread across the floor, I stare at the pale, dead body before me. Fear, anger and happiness spread inside me. Fear of someone finding the body, anger of the fact that the body is going to get me caught, happiness at the fact she is dead. The questions going through my mind are, how am I going to get away with it? No one ever comes up to this old house, it's been abandoned for years. Will they have search parties? Will the police get involved? Will I be charged for murder, for murdering my own step-sister?

Well it's her fault, she should never have come here with her father, she shouldn't have stolen my friends or my boyfriend, most of all she shouldn't have stolen my mum. She was all I had left in the world. What am I going to do? There is too much evidence; I am going to get caught. There are footprints, fingerprints, hairs, I couldn't go back home. I couldn't run away. One thought ran through my mind, one thought that could solve all my problems, one thought where I will never have to go to jail. I once read, one life for another, I never really understood it till now. So, once again I looked at the black monster in my hand, pulled the trigger.

Bang! Darkness.

Kirsty Buckley (12)
St Julie's High School, Woolton

A Day In The Life Of Mary White

Today is the worst day of my life! I'm lying here, in my bed crying, and not knowing what to do. You're probably wondering why. I'll tell you.

Yesterday, I was in school. The weather was scorching, and I was looking forward to going home to play with my dog, Mixy. 3.30pm came, and as soon as I knew it, I was on the bus home. Also, it was Friday, so I was extra excited. The bus journey seemed to drag, it was so crowded on there, I felt the sweat dripping down my brow.

Finally, it came to my stop, but I had to squeeze my way through what seemed like hundreds of people. When I got off the bus, I had to walk down the road to my house.

When I arrived, it seemed ever so quiet. I peeped through my back gate, the dog wasn't running around and my sister wasn't on the trampoline. It was very strange. I opened the door and my sister was crying. I asked her what was wrong, but I couldn't work out what she was saying, and that was the moment my mother told me Mixy was dead.

So, this leaves me back here - in my bed. She died very suddenly - of old age. It's just because she's been with our family for five years. I'll have to try and come to terms with her death. I don't know what I'm going to do without her.

Lucy Morgan (13)
St Julie's High School, Woolton

A Day In The Life Of Steven Gerrard

Running on the pitch at the start of the first half, my heart starts to race. I look around, tension's in the air, a fantastic atmosphere is flying around Anfield and the crowds are in the middle of the chorus of 'You'll Never Walk Alone'. The whistle blows and the nerves disappear, nothing is on my mind but to win this game and determination fills up my body. Six minutes gone and the crowd fires up! Was it in? Nobody either knows or cares. A smile creeps upon my face as half-time is reached but the fans are in a more confident mood than we are.

As I walk back onto the pitch, however, confidence fills my body and we are off once again. Ninety minutes up, but extra time still rattles on. Gasps across the Kop as a shot from Chelsea skims the post. The whole stadium impatiently waiting for the six added minutes to conclude. My muscles are aching and I stand breathless as the ball gets passed from one to another, wasting the time. The crowds biting their nails in anxiety. The final whistle sounds, a sudden adrenaline rush hits me. Ear-piercing roars from the fans. The players are ecstatic. One-nil ... just about, but we are off to Istanbul!

Gabriella Langton (13)
St Julie's High School, Woolton

A Day In The Life Of Sophina-Marie

There I was, walking home from school like I did every day. Nothing unusual or out of place could be seen, so you can imagine how shocked I was when I found myself being grabbed by the arm and bundled into a van like a few bags of rubbish. I sat there, in this rather large, foul smelling van with my hands tied together behind me, with an extremely strong piece of rope. I was covered in bruises as well, after being knocked around so much.

I was just thinking about my family at the time, when I found myself being yanked out of the van and hauled into a small box room blanketed with dust. I didn't know where I was but I knew that if I stayed there, I wouldn't last long.

Finally, I saw the man who had kidnapped me. He was absolutely disgusting, he had clumps of food stuck in his beard and desperately needed a shave, he also wore a rather large, dark blue bobble hat. *This man needs a wash,* was my first thought, he had an awful smell lingering over him and I was terrified.

What was I to do? I needed to get away, but I then realised that I would never be able to. I screamed, so he put a rope around my throat and tied it, I screamed again, that was a stupid mistake, I screamed once more and he pulled it tighter and tighter and tighter and tighter and then, it stopped ...

Nicola Heywood (13)
St Julie's High School, Woolton

The Sapphire-Eyed Princess

I knew that things were too good to be true. All of my people in India had gathered in my stunning palace in celebration of my coronation. My beautiful daughter, whom I loved very much, was dancing joyfully, her glittering sapphire eyes shone as brightly as the stars.

Later, a piercing scream broke the happiness of the great feast.

'Your highness, a fire has started in your palace!' Before I could respond, I was whisked away by my guards. I gasped in terror as I watched my palace being traded for ashes. Then I suddenly realised, 'Where is ...?' I didn't pause to complete my sentence.

'Save her! Save my daughter!' I was held firmly back, as I wept and screamed, I knew it was too late.

The sounds of people shouting depressed me. Then, strangely, a crowd started patting me, I didn't need to wonder why. I couldn't accept that my beautiful sapphire-eyed daughter was gone forever.

Now, many years later, I am still trying to overcome the grief. The sapphires on my necklace all remind me of the same terrible story. I am drawing and will continue to drown in my own ocean of tears and sorrow, I will remain taunted by the terrible memories the jewels contain. As I watch the crowning of a new young, beautiful queen, I still think that my daughter should be there.

Rebecca Grundy (13)
St Julie's High School, Woolton

The Day In The Life Of A World War Two Soldier

As I scurry frantically through the mud-filled trenches my heart is racing so fast that I feel it will burst through my chest. The rain falls heavily from the sky, the air is so foggy that I cannot see my hand in front of my face and the noise so loud that my ears are ringing.

Walking through the trenches stepping over the dead corpses lying there in a heap on the floor the stench is unbearable. Another man goes down, cries of pain and agony are coming out from every angle. I carry my rifle close to my chest shooting aimlessly towards the enemy. Then I realise that I have run out of ammunition and my rifle is empty. I know now that the only way I will survive is if I crawl along the floor of the trenches in the mud. I sink into it face first countless numbers of times.

Suddenly I felt a sharp pain in my left arm and my chest. I look down and see a patch of blood. I scream out loud then throw myself to the ground in pain, gradually sinking down further and further into the mud of the trench, I can feel my heart going slower and slower. My head, hands and toes go numb and I cannot feel anything. I cry out for the last time, feeling immense pain, knowing that I have just moments left to live. I think about my family to try to block out the agony I am undergoing, then finally, I take one last breath, close my eyes and feel my heart beat its last.

Sian Penny (12)
St Julie's High School, Woolton

In The Moonlight Forever?

Moonlight beams dancing on the canopy of the trees, reflecting from the crystal ball held by the delicate, nimble hands of a flying fairy. Her black, long hair and blue eyes shine brightly in the moonlight. Moondust is sprinkling out from the invisible wings, silence as she flutters in the air except for the wind whispering her name, 'Eclipsa'.

As the moon's rays began to fade a mass of orange, red and yellow flooding the sky, makes Eclipsa fly suddenly to her closing moonlight drop. In her hurry, through the grass, she got caught by a flying, humming, yellow and black rush. The bee flying in and out of all the forest of grass, as it quickly brushes past pastures of floral outbursts, Eclipsa tumbled into an opened bud.

Feeling the fierce, bright, red-hot sun burning her pale skin, she leaned out of this unusual flower, finding herself drop to the ground. Covering herself in mud, her hair no longer shines and when she attempts to fly, her bent wing prevents her from getting anywhere.

Suddenly, she gets attacked with a flurry of fairies' wings whacking her. She began to fall, when he came flying down with an arrogant look on his face and dressed in bright yellow leaves and fiery red hair. In the morning rush, his name could be heard being called, 'Soleil'.

Finding herself alone and in shadows, she is exhausted and lost ready to rest.

Awoken by the whispers of the wind ...

Charlotte Bell (12)
St Julie's High School, Woolton

Final Day In The Life Of Patch

She doesn't have time to hug, stroke and love me. Shelley only loves Fluff ...

For example, the time she gave Fluff a kiss and said, 'You'll always be my favourite,' and she kicked me in the stomach.

'Oh Patch, you really are the cutest dog!' said Shelley's mum constantly. But I only want Shelley's attention like the old days, how it used to be before Fluff came along.

'But Mum, Fluff is a newborn puppy! She needs to be looked after extra-specially! Patch is just an old scraggy dog!'

The words repeated in my head; *old scraggy dog, old scraggy dog.*

Just like you used to look after me extra-specially, I thought. And when Fluff glanced at me with a smug and satisfied look in Shelley's arms, whilst I was sitting in the corner of the room on a cardboard box, I knew something had to be done.

I could not bark and expect people to understand, but I could get my message across in other ways; I did not want to break Shelley's heart - so I could not consider getting rid of Fluff, so I decided I'd do something else ...

So here I am, on the road, where the van hit me, and I finally know where I belong now; unlike not knowing where I belonged with Shelley. I am going to go and take a last glance at my family, and go where I will be happy ...

... Heaven.

Lorna Quail (13)
St Julie's High School, Woolton

A Day In The Life Of Trudy Brown

It's very, very cold. It's very, very creepy. But for me it's home and where I belong. The cellar! I can guess what you're thinking now, *what kind of child lives in a cellar?* But I think nothing of it as I have now lived here for 3 years. Ever since my parents died and the lady over the road brought me to this private school.

The reason I have the cellar whilst the other sixteen children have their own bedrooms covered with toys and decorated just the way they want it, is because orphans don't have parents or family to pay the fees so the cellar is my home.

Really I should be grateful because if they hadn't brought me here I'd be homeless.

So another day begins and my usual routine takes place. Firstly I wake up at five and make a packed lunch for each child. This takes about one hour as there are sixteen sandwiches and sixteen of everything. Then I iron all sixteen uniforms and make sixteen breakfasts. My tired feet climb the winding staircase of this Victorian house to start the rest of my daily chores. The other children go to classes with their friends, something I don't have, as my dad was my only friend. I tell myself, *you should always be grateful for what you have.*

This is what my mother used to tell me. Oh what I'd give to hear her say that just one more time.

Charlotte McCombs (13)
St Julie's High School, Woolton

A Day In The Life Of Jane Smith

I sat down on the hard, cold floor, staring into the darkness and listening to the faint sounds of screaming in the distance. Shaking, I put my face in my hands, closed my eyes tight and wished this was all a dream, that I would wake up in my lovely warm bedroom in a friendly atmosphere, instead of this dark, cold, dingy room that I was locked in.

As time went on, the screams grew nearer and I shivered, thinking of what my punishment would be, for being different. What I would be pressured into doing. How I would be victimised. After the intense wait, my time came. The door in front of me unlocked. Three big, stocky men stood in front of me, smirking and armed with different weapons each - a rope, a knife and a pair of scissors. I dreaded to think of what would happen next.

The only sounds around me were my heavy breathing and the sound of one of the men's footsteps coming towards me. I froze in fear. The man blindfolded me so I could see nothing. I heard the men muttering to each other, then footsteps coming towards me. Then I felt pain and terror. I tried screaming for help, but no sound came out. The men left me and walked away, laughing. I tried moving. I couldn't. I was too weak. The only sound in the room was my breathing and eventually that stopped, along with my heart. My life was over but at least I was free from all the pain and terror.

Rachel Murray (13)
St Julie's High School, Woolton

The Warning

It was a normal day for Will Scot in London's harbour, as usual Will went down to the local bar to gamble.

As soon as he entered the bar a rush of alcohol and smoke brushed past his nose.

Will sat down self-assured, knowing he was going to win the poker game and the two tickets for a journey on the great Titanic.

20 minutes passed and Will won the poker game, he walked out proudly with the tickets.

Will ran off in anticipation to go on the Titanic with his friend Thomas. As they were running Will heard a thousand screams of terror, he turned round but nothing was stirring, all was calm, he carried on walking.

At last Will and Thomas were on the magnificent Titanic sailing to America.

The Titanic was halfway across the Atlantic, Will was asleep. He had a dream that terrified him, in it was an odd looking man saying, 'Turn back, turn back while you can!' Will woke up pouring with sweat, he decided to go up on deck. As he reached the top of the deck an iceberg was plunging towards him.

Before Will could turn the iceberg hit the Titanic, the Titanic snapped. Will plunged to his death, into the icy-cold sea, never to see the light of day again.

Libby Coulter (13)
St Julie's High School, Woolton

The Warning

It was early Sunday afternoon and I decided to go on MSN to talk to my friends. Faye signed in and started the conversation, I was talking to her for a while then all of a sudden the screen went blank. After a few minutes, the screen appeared again and she told me a close relative was going to die in a serious accident. I asked her how did she know this, but all she was saying was, 'I am telling you the truth,' then she left the conversation.

I approached her in the playground in school the next day about the worrying conversation we had Sunday afternoon. She denied it all and she told me she had gone for a meal with her family on Sunday.

It slipped my mind after that, I just thought it must have been a silly person playing a joke on me.

I went home as normal that day but no one appeared to be home, it wasn't like Mum not to tell me she was going out. As I watched television there was a phone call, it was Mum. She sounded distraught, she told me there had been an accident and there was some bad news. My nine-year-old cousin had been coming home from school and had been knocked down by a lorry, she had lived for several hours then sadly passed away.

Suzanne Brodie (13)
St Julie's High School, Woolton

The Magnet

Margaret and Jane were friends for a number of years and helped each other through thick and thin. In 1966 Jane went on holiday to Spain for a short break, after a week Jane came back with a small souvenir; a fridge magnet in the shape of a cow.

Jane was a very heavy smoker and smoked about fifty cigarettes a day, Margaret was constantly trying to encourage Jane to stop and always reminded her about the threats of cancer.

But Jane never took any notice. In July 1967, Jane was rushed into hospital, at the same time the magnet fell off the fridge and smashed in a number of places.

Later on that day Jane was diagnosed with cancer and was allowed home after a couple of weeks to break the painful news to Margaret. They had a very serious talk and Margaret took the news pretty well and promised Jane that she would get through this. Jane was very ill for a number of months and again the magnet fell off the fridge and smashed, a couple of hours later Jane was read her last rites and died on her sick bed.

Margaret took this sign as a blessing, letting her now that Jane was soon to be accepted into Heaven.

Faye Aldridge (12)
St Julie's High School, Woolton

The Warning

Tom packed the last of his clothes into his suitcase then sat down to watch television. There was a news broadcast; two planes had just crashed into the Twin Towers in New York. He turned off the television. He was scared because the day after he was going to be flying to New York with his girlfriend Carol. Tom rang his mum to tell her what he had just seen on television, she didn't know anything about it, she hadn't watched the news all day.

At the airport Tom was nervous of going, after what he had seen on the television. Carol noticed that he was acting very strangely. Tom asked Carol if she had seen the news yesterday about the plane crash in New York. She said she was watching the news all day and nothing like that came on. She thought Tom was joking because he knew she was scared of flying. Tom was really confused, why was he the only one who had seen the broadcast?

As they were in the air, a man pulled out his gun and said he was going to take over the plane and crash it into the Twin Towers. Tom had an idea what might happen because of what he had seen on the news. Tom texted his mum saying the man had taken over the plane and was going to fly it into one of the Twin Towers, 'I love you and I will see you in Heaven.'

Siobhan White (13)
St Julie's High School, Woolton

The Warning

I was so upset when my cousin died in a car crash. I was devastated. She was older than me and like an older sister.

A week ago strange things started happening to me. Like when I went to cross the road and my mobile phone rang, as I stopped to answer it a car came racing down the road, lost control and crashed. My heart was beating like someone was pounding on a drum.

Another time was when I was lost in Liverpool city centre, I had a text message on my phone saying, 'Follow sign Clayton Square.' I was scared because I did not know who it was from. When I followed the signs, I knew where I was and was not lost anymore.

When I got home that night I realised it had been twice in the week that I had been saved from something bad happening to me. 'If somebody is helping me, show me a sign,' I said, hoping for a reply, then a teddy fell off the top of the wardrobe. I replied, 'Who are you?' A name came on my noticeboard saying, 'Natasha', next to it in brackets was '(your cousin)'.

I did not feel scared, just happy and comforted that I knew she was still looking after me even though she was dead. Although I was still a little sad because I realised what a lovely, thoughtful cousin I had lost.

Rachel Prayle (12)
St Julie's High School, Woolton

The Messages

She thought her life was perfect until she moved to Cherrywood Avenue.

Rebecca recently moved to Cherrywood Avenue, she thought it would be a happy road, but that was about to change. Rebecca had made a few new friends from the road. She decided to text her new mate she had met to come round to get to know her better. Whilst her mate was there she had asked her if she had heard about 'Murdered Megan', she said no and her mate told her the story.

Megan was a happy girl but one night when she arrived home her mother wasn't well. Megan's room was in the attic and Megan had fallen asleep, her mother then crept in and murdered Megan but no one knows how.

Rebecca did not sleep that night, she thought, *it can't be true,* but then she suddenly received a text message saying, 'It's true'. Rebecca thought that her mate was messing with her but her mate was asleep because she had rung her.

Rebecca's mum was in work until 12 so she thought she would go up to Megan's room and see what her room was like. Rebecca quietly opened the door and crept into the room, it felt damp and smelt funny. She saw nothing. She then got another text saying, 'I have just seen you, luv Megan xx.'

Rebecca ran down the stairs and pretended she never received the text. Rebecca went to great her breakfast. Every morning she had jam on toast. Rebecca then received another text saying, 'I like jam on toast too!' Rebecca slowly walked back in fright.

Katherine Barr (13)
St Julie's High School, Woolton

The Decision

It was just a normal evening at first for Jacob, he was sitting at his desk signing contracts for parliament, when he heard a bleeping noise coming from his mobile phone. He walked over and found it was a message. It said, 'We know what you have been up to.' At first he didn't panic, but then he received another. 'Change your mind, or else.' Jacob began to panic, his palms were sweaty and his legs were as shaky as a newborn animal.

After a while Jacob took no notice to these messages and stuck with his decision to go to war. Then more warning messages were received. This time to tell him that his plan for war will backfire. 'Beware, take cover you will not escape!'

At the same time that Jacob got these messages his television changed channel and showed the futuristic outcome of the decision to go to war.

The television showed images of what would happen at war. Women, children and families would be torn apart, businesses would be destroyed and a terrible hardship would overcome all those affected.

After this terrifying ordeal, Jacob thought long and hard about what was best for his country. Then he received another message saying, 'Keep thinking, keep thinking, beware!'

After these worrying messages Jacob decided that it was not in the best interests of the world to go to war. As a result no further messages were received, but will he receive more when he makes other decisions?

Ashleigh-Jane Bauress (13)
St Julie's High School, Woolton

The Spiral Stairs

It was just an ordinary school day until me and my friend found out some exciting news. All that day there was a rumour going around about a set of spiral stairs in an old closet hidden away.

Not only that but rumour has it that a nun once pushed a girl down many years ago and they've been blocked off ever since. So the two of us decided to meet back there at 3.30.

3.30 came, the school was abandoned so we secretly snuck back. Me and Rachel looked at each other in excitement, then I slowly pushed the door open. The door creaked to reveal an old cleaner's closet, but as we slowly peered around the corner we saw a rusty set of spiral stairs.

Suddenly the door was slammed shut and a key turned in the door. We both leapt for the door to try and unlock it. There was no use though. So I desperately tried my mobile but all I kept getting was a mysterious text message saying, 'Get out!' which started to scare me.

Eventually, we decided that the only chance of escaping would be to go down the stairs. Rachel took the first step down. I followed her and took hold of the icy banister. Then slowly we went deeper and deeper, keeping close together.

It was almost pitch-black so I took out my torch. We carried on till … 'Argh!' screamed Rachel.

I looked round frantically for her but she had gone! The hairs on my back stood up and my heart raced. I quickly took out my mobile phone and started to type in the number when something knocked it out of my hand.

I froze with fear. Then when I turned around … *'Help!'*

Christine Dempsey (13)
St Julie's High School, Woolton

Ghostly Fears

One summer's night last year, I was on my computer in my bedroom, Mum was watching television and my sister Amelia was asleep.

In school that day Kasey told me about a website called 'Ghostly' where you would see pictures and videos of ghosts. So I went on it and watched a video of a ghost in a dark bedroom, but it wasn't that frightening, so I watched one which said *'Warning'* on it. As the video went on, I didn't like what I was watching, so I turned my computer off and went to sleep.

In the middle of the night I kept waking up thinking of the video, my heart started to beat like a leopard running so fast it could take off any second, my neck began to sweat anxiously. As I looked around my bedroom that's when I saw ... a huge ghostly figure on the screen of my computer, whispering something, which I couldn't quite hear because I was breathing so heavy. As the whisper changed to a yell I suddenly heard what it was shouting. 'Kill yourself, before someone else does.'

That's when I thought I was dreaming, but a very horrible dream, I hid under my quilt screaming, then my mum came running in wondering why my computer was on and why I was yelling. But there was no use telling her because she wouldn't understand.

In the morning I woke and noticed the empty paracetamol bottle. Was that what sent me to sleep?

Elly Roche (13)
St Julie's High School, Woolton

Unlucky 13th

It was a dark and stormy night and the wind was blowing hard on the windows and windchimes. It was Friday the 13th and Melanie and her friends were alone in the house and thought it would be a fun thing to do to play the Ouija board. They set it all out and connected with a young boy called Ben, aged five. He asked them to set him free. They did but when he was free he said he wasn't really a young boy of five, he was an evil spirit. Melanie and her friends noticed the lights were flickering on and off. Then they heard a bleep on the phone. Melanie got it out of her pocket, her hand shaking. She opened up the message, it said, 'You will die!' 150 times recurring. Melanie noticed her friends had gone.

Melanie started to shiver with fear. She decided to phone someone but had realised the phone had gone dead. Then she tried to get out of the doors and windows but they had been locked and bolted. Melanie decided that she was being paranoid but was still a bit shaken up. She put the radio on. It crackled and then a song came on. It was called, 'It's your time to go'. Melanie didn't realise this was a message and just carried on listening. There was a bang and then all black. Melanie saw a white light and flashbacks from her life and then all of a sudden blackness.

Sarah Wakefield (13)
St Julie's High School, Woolton

A Day In The Life Of Pounce

Today was it, I had eight lives left and I had a feeling in my stomach, I knew this was the day that I would lose my nine lives. I also thought it was hunger, I was right as I heard my strange two-legged owner call me, 'Pounce' as he did every day at seven o'clock.

After I had walked over like a snail to enjoy my meal of tuna, the strange feeling came back, and this time I definitely knew it was the end for me.

As I ran down the road as fast as my short legs would take me, the scrumptious smell of the fishmongers across the road wafted up my nose and seemed to carry me over to it. I entered and pounced up at the fish and the usual two-legged thing was behind the counter and he threw me a big tuna fish over and I caught it with my old torn away teeth. Then I scampered out and gobbled up the fish.

I slowly frisked home back up the road feeling as joyful as ever, but then something happened, I was picked up and put into a bag by another of those two-legged people and they took me down to the canal, as I could hear the ducks, and threw me into it.

After a couple of hours or so I woke in a strange place, and I didn't feel well at all and all of a sudden I collapsed ...

Sarah Clutton (13)
St Julie's High School, Woolton

A Day In The Life Of Margaret Maloney

'My darling Margaret,

It has been six weeks; four days since I last took a glance at your remarkable face and I tell you one thing, I miss you awfully ...'

This was the beginning of a long, gloomy letter from my brave, courageous husband who is doing his duty for our country in the war.

You see, I know he has to do it as he has no choice, but I am worried sick. Every time I hear the news; somebody or should I say some people have died or a soldier has been badly injured, I can't help feeling uneasy as all my thoughts are of Dave.

The days are dragging, minutes seem like hours and hours seem like days. Here I am alone, with my devoted husband thousands of miles away, I am terrified. During this idiotic war I have already lost some of my family members, my mum, dad, sister and brother. Can my life get any worse?

Sirens, bombs, planes are all I seem to hear but to think that Dave is in danger is unbearable, why do bad things happen to me? I am so scared; all I seem to be doing is glancing up at the subdued and gloomy sky, wondering how I could be experiencing this disaster alone. I miss familiar faces and things around me, I feel isolated. I only see people when I go to the air raid shelter and that makes me feel even worse as the smell there is the most obnoxious smell I have ever experienced in my life.

All I can do is pray!

Kirsty Wall (13)
St Julie's High School, Woolton

A Day In The Life Of A Fox

I'm trapped! What if they hurt me? What will my cubs do without me? I've got to get out! Somebody help me! How did I let myself get into this situation?

I'd set out to find some food for me and my cubs, we hadn't eaten for a couple of days and the cubs were crying. I was weak with hunger as well. I had to find something to eat soon. I went out of the gate and was walking along the road when I saw a patch of grass that looked very comfortable, so I sat down thinking I'd just have a little rest, and I must have fallen asleep.

Now, how will I get out of this situation? All the humans, are looking at me, coming in on me, they are going to hurt me. My life flashing before my eyes, my cubs, my home, me! The cars nearby are zooming past. How will I get home safely? The noise sounds like waves crashing against rocks. I have to get out now, I have to take a chance.

I dash across the road just about missing the steady flow of cars. Then across the pavement and jumping onto the gate, just missing the bars.

I'm safe, back in my home, my field, there are no humans here, just me and my cubs, safe, together, no cars or noise, nothing. Relief floods over me like a warm blanket.

Olivia Hobson (13)
St Julie's High School, Woolton

An Extract From 'A Day In The Life Of Ellen'

Beep! Beep! went Ellen's alarm clock. She staggered out of bed and started to look for it. *Beep! Beep!* The alarm clock carried on. *Oh where are you?* Ellen thought to herself. At last she found it. Then she went in search of a cup to make herself a cup of tea. Whilst she was looking for the cup she heard scratching. Curious of what it was she went to look and found out that it was her cat, Tom. 'Miaow,' went the cat.

'What's up?' asked Ellen, 'are you hungry?' She forgot about her cup of tea and started looking for some food for Tom. 'It looks like I've run out of it,' she said to the cat, 'I'll have to go out for some, but I'll have to be quick because I can't be late for work again.' She ran for her coat and rushed to the shop.

Ellen had a job in the vet's, looking after all of the lost animals. She had to be in on time though because for the past few mornings she had been late and was scared of getting fired. She finally got home and poured out Tom's food. She looked at the clock and said to herself, *Is that what time it is? I'm going to be late.* She rushed up the stairs to get ready.

Just as she reached the front door the phone rang. *I'll have to leave it*, she said to herself, *I'm already late as it is.*

When she finally reached work her friend, Holly, said to her, 'Are you OK? You look a bit pale.'

'I'm fine,' replied Ellen, 'I've just rushed around too much this morning.' She got on with her work duties; cleaning, feeding and caring for all of the animals.

At last it was 6 o'clock in the evening. *Great, now I can go home* she thought to herself. She grabbed her coat and headed home. When she arrived home she heard the television on. *That's funny, I know that I switched it off this morning*, she thought ...

Natalie Jones (12)
Shorefields Technology College

Pandora's Box

On the island of Cyprus, in the middle of the Greek Empire, lived a girl called Pandora. Pandora was a normal girl with beautiful long flowing brown hair and lovely turquoise eyes. Everybody who was anybody knew Pandora. However, in a matter of days Pandora's life was changed from normal to very abstract.

One day whilst walking, Pandora stumbled across a dark and mysterious cave. Being the nosy type Pandora decided to enter the peculiarly placed cave, even after warnings concerning a hungry Cyclops. As Pandora walked ever further into the darkening cave, she could hear faint whispers tickling her eardrums. A blinding light was pushing her to the end of the winding cave. Pandora ran to what she thought to be an exit. She ran and ran as if running to the mainland, the light getting ever brighter.

Pandora ending her race with light entered a large arched cave. Stood in the middle was a large podium with a heavily decorated box sat on the top. With the whispers beating across her ear, Pandora stepped up to the box her hands falling over the sides. The whispers continued to become deafening and as Pandora lifted the box, the cave walls started to crumble, and as quick as light Pandora fled.

When Pandora finally reached her home, she locked all her doors and fell into the corner of her main room. She placed the box a foot away, Pandora's eyes were fixed on a lid, her fingers reached towards the handle, she grasped it and held it as if she was clinging to life itself. Slowly she opened the box ...

Tom Evans (14)
The Mosslands School

A Day In The Life Of Lou From Little Britain

As usual woke up and went for morning run, came back and had a small breakfast, as I ate my breakfast I cried as I thought about having to watch monster trucks with Andy for the millionth time.

Went round to Andy's at 8.00 and woke him up. After several attempts I finally got him into his wheelchair and went to make his breakfast, when I came back I found Andy back in bed. Confused for rest of day.

Made Andy breakfast in bed, after finishing he asks for second one. After Andy's third and fourth, we went for our morning walk. Stop to get Andy an ice cream from shop. After an argument with man behind till about the earliness of the ice cream, get hit in face. Tell Andy he can't have an ice cream, talk to someone I know, come back, see assistant slumped over the desk, run in and take ice cream, come back, give Andy ice cream, says he doesn't want it.

Eat ice cream, get Andy another. Take him home, make his many lunches. Go to pub for date, Andy rings my mobile asking for a monster truck video, tell date, she slaps me for lying. Come out pub with black eye and mark on face. Arrive at Andy's for tea bringing chippy with me. Go out 10 minutes later for second chippy with ice cream.

Watch monster trucks for six hours praying to God that it will end soon. Leave Andy's, after tucking him in, reading a book about monster trucks three times and giving him another ice cream. Go home and cry myself to sleep.

Neil Harper (13)
The Mosslands School

The War Of The Worlds

In the land of Kelfa everything was peaceful until one day the dreaded Syranni invaded, in their quest for world domination.

Chapter 8 - Under Fire!

Wave after wave of Syranni crashed against the mighty walls of the great fortress. For miles on end Syranni soldiers charged, crashing into the walls with tremendous force. For three years the red and white of the Syranni warriors had pounded the gates of the great city. Over the last few days the assault had increased in fierceness.

'General, General, there is a martial of dark elves north of the forest,' one of the young patrollers said in a mid sprint.

'Elves ... north of the forest? This cannot be right, the elves have not ventured north of their forest for centuries. It is their homeland.' General Ty replied in a worried voice with an expression of fear and bewilderment on his face.

'General we need more men on the north wall, they are being overrun.'

'Send a batch of the reserves over there. This castle has withstood worse attacks than that of a war-obsessed race of thugs and pirates. Ethan send your scouts out to find out what has frightened the elves.'

'Of course General, yes Sir.'

Boom!

'What the ... the mountain!'

All fighting stopped as Syranni and Kelfineans stood side by side to check out what had created the deafening noise from the mountain.

All went silent as the mountain continued to explode in random places. Sending huge missiles of rocks and boulders into the midst of the battle. Then from over the top of the mountain a gleam of gold and white. ... it was amazing. It was as if the Earth stood still as from over the mountain one of the most beautifully created creatures appeared in the blue of the sky.

Steven Griffiths (14)
The Mosslands School

North-West Infested By Locusts

Yesterday the north-west began to feel the damage and distress caused by the building-eating, locust-like creatures that have recently infested Southport. The public have had to be evacuated from their own homes. Pleasureland has been dominated by these nuisance creatures. The locusts have dominated Southport Pleasureland and are now advancing on to parts of Neston.

The locusts have come from North Africa and have now become accustomed to cool weather and more food to eat.

'It was horrible, I was moved away from my home in Neston and all my belongings were left there. I stayed at my friend's house and I watched my house get destroyed by a swarm of locusts on the television,' said Dr Tina Upton, a victim of the locusts.

It has been predicted by the council that within three days the city of Liverpool will be gone. At the town hall in Seacombe, there has been a model created for the simulation of this pest epidemic. It showed what was going to happen ... everything you can imaging will be gone ... St John's Beacon, the Liver Buildings. We desperately need help. Pest control teams from all over the UK have been trying to conquer these creatures but all has failed, the rain hasn't even stopped them yet. Police have been very helpful in keeping people calm, this must be greatly appreciated.

Continued on page 2.

Philip Jones (14)
The Mosslands School

Dragon Of The Mountain

As the proud Greeks marched in their battle-line towards the enemy, the crows circled overhead, eager for flesh. The usual brightness of the Persian army was diminished and swallowed by the massive rock. As the Greeks entered the mountain's shadow rank by rank, the sun stopped glinting off their hoplon shields and their Corinthian helmets like a bulb gone out. The hordes of Persia faced the organised, ordered Greek army. The pikes lowered to form the infamous Phalanx. The horns of both nations rung out across the vast plains, and the armies clashed. The onslaught of Persia was terrible, but the well choreographed and rehearsed Greek fighting style was presenting a stalemate. After an hour the men were weary. The mountain presented itself majestically, but both sides felt uncomfortable in its presence.

Suddenly, from the heart of the mountain there came a hollow roar, as if it were roared in a vast empty cavern. The sounds bounced around the plains like a ball against a wall, and with a clash of metal, the fighting stopped. The Greek's bronze armour was clanking madly as the Earth shook. The side of the mountain exploded in a horrible yell. As the creature flew from the gap, its scales were shiny yet not reflective, its roar empty, yet full, its wings were vast, they could have enveloped the whole of the field, the eyes were alight, yet dark, it was a draining light, and as the dragon bore down on its prey, the sarrisa spears of Greece cracked before it, then the field was black.

James Ferrier (14)
The Mosslands School

Part Of A Short Story

This part of a short story tells the events of when the, purely fictional, corpse of Sir Geoffrey was discovered. This piece is meant to have taken place after the usual dinner party the previous night and before the discovery of the murderer.

Radcliffe Manor awoke to the sound of a scream coming from Mary Terrence, the housekeeper.

The scream awoke all of the guests. One of the guests who had been awoken was Major Robert Banks, the sixty-something, well-dressed, much respected dear friend to the Manor's owner, Sir Geoffrey Radcliffe.

He quickly arose, throwing a smart dressing gown over himself, fetching his pistol from where it sat in his suitcase (which ever since the Great War he refused to travel without) and walked briskly towards the direction from which the scream came.

He discovered the cook had fainted and she lay in the corridor, the door to Radcliffe's room stood ajar. Anna, one of the maids came running down the corridor.

'Look after her my girl,' he spoke to the maid who did as she was told, despite being extremely frightened both by the sight of her friend Mary unconscious on the floor and over the Major armed with a gun.

Banks loaded the gun and then burst through the door, horrified at the sight that met his eyes.

Lying face up at the foot of the grand mahogany bed was his dear senescent friend Sir Geoffrey Radcliffe, though his appearance had changed somewhat since the dinner party the night before. He was gagged with one of his silk handkerchiefs, a dagger was impaled in his abdomen. He lay in a pool of his own blood, face gaunt with an expression of grave fear. His dear friend had been horrifically murdered.

Peter Joad (14)
The Mosslands School

Plane Disaster

It was a nice sunny day on the last week of school. Only I wasn't in school but on a plane laughing evily to myself at my friends. We were going on holiday to Australia where my uncle Joe lives. Every year we went over there to see him.

As the flight progressed it got colder and colder and the plane kept shuddering violently. We were reminded time and time again that it was a bit of turbulence, but I got the feeling there was something about to go horribly wrong. One of the passengers got up from his seat, barging his way past the air-hostess and breaking into the pilot's room.

In an angry, loud voice we heard the man say, 'I used to be a pilot and a plane isn't supposed to shake this much, what's going on?' Then we heard a small, squeaky voice and a minute later we heard the pilot's voice through the speakers.

'This is your pilot speaking, we are flying directly over a tornado. This shouldn't affect the flight and this plane will continue to its destination.'

Moments later we heard a loud crash from the room in front of us. Screams of horror emitted from the room and I could hear a strange mixture of creaking metal and what sounded like strong wind. In shock one of the passengers ran to the emergency door and wrenched it open. The plane groaned and began to collapse. It was like being in a can while it was being crushed. Suddenly I felt my life creep away.

Michael Cropper (14)
The Mosslands School

A Bloody Good Dinner

Crime in London is at its highest peak, behind all the murders, drug smuggling and kidnappings is crime lord Eskibob Supple. It is only when Mr Supple has his portrait painted by a rather charming gentleman that crime in London dramatically reduces. But who is this anonymous painter, and why has crime suddenly decreased?

The portrait of Eskibob Supple was almost complete. The painting looked exactly like him, big nose, scarred chin and the biggest glass eye I'd ever seen, the fact the eye was not his, but one of his former colleagues just added to the intensity of the man, despite being the crime lord of London, the man was feeble and slimy, he slobbered constantly and stuttered on the odd occasion.

'Complete,' I said over the top of the easel.

'Oh, good,' he replied, he stood up and came over to me.

'Would you like to join me for dinner tonight, in celebration of my portrait's completion?'

'Of course,' I lied. 'I recommend the Silver Rose, I have been there on my last few meals, and been pleasantly surprised.'

'Yes certainly, eight o'clock suit you?' I nodded and walked with him to the door, we both said goodbye and he left.

I had arranged for us to sit in a secluded area where we would be alone. When we both arrived we sat down and ordered our meal, Mavis was called over and served us our champagne and Supple's waffling began. By the time we had reached the fish dish I was tired of his foolish stories and violent antics so I did the decent thing and shot him.

I stood up, wiped my mouth and began to walk out. Mavis walked in, 'Would you like me to clean up Sir?'

'If you would please Mavis.'

Alex Kewin (14)
The Mosslands School

Blood Thirst

Cast down from power by a haunting glyph knight centuries ago, Melkiah awakens in a world he barely recognises. His armies slain and his brethren nearly extinct, Melkiah is among the last of his kind. Driven by vengeance, Melkiah shall unleash a vicious wrath to uncover the plot that threatens the land he seeks to conquer.

From the shards of twisted dreams I rose - unwilling.

Tossed upon tides of agonising pain that flowed and ebbed and left me searingly awake. And more revoltingly - alive.

It was then I saw her for the first time.

A woman stood in the doorway, leaning against the frame with the sunset behind her. She was quite clearly a vampire.

'Good evening. We did not expect you to awaken so soon. Already you surprise us.'

My mind was in fragments like shattered glass. 'Where am I? I-I don't remember.'

'Yes, it was said your memory would be affected by your long slumber. That will pass, in time. I am Surel, and I am here to help you. Know that your name is Melkiah, and you were once a power in the land.'

I rose from the bed. 'I know my name. But my past - I remember fragments only.'

'That you awoke at all is a miracle. When we found you, there was but the barest thread of life in you. We nurtured it, fed it, and now you rise and walk again.'

'And what is this place?'

'You are in the city of Meridian, capital of the land of Malroth, the land you once sought to conquer and rule. Tell me, since you remember your name, do you also remember your nature?'

I stretched my jaw to reveal my long blood-stained fangs, 'Of course.'

I followed her out onto the balcony and looked upon an unrecognisable Meridian with its dirty streets and peasant infestation. It would once again be glorious under my rule.

Tom O'Brien (14)
The Mosslands School

Brothers Of The Skies

In a land where heroes are made, two brothers, Arithnon and Hesus are subject to a cruel infirmity of the gods. Their trial lasts for their whole lives and in the end claims them and they are disembowelled, by a creature with awesome power.

Before time had any real meaning Greece was plagued with an array of mythical creatures. All creations of the gods. These legends preyed upon the mortal and cursed them, eternally.

Hesus and Arithnon spent their days like any other children, getting into mischief and basking in the ferocious glare of the sun. Today was the 3rd of the 3rd, and just like any other day the market was in hype, with shoppers hurriedly scurrying across scorched sand to a destination with no value.

A bead of sweat coursed its way down Arithnon's cheek as he clambered up the crevice of the rock face. Their parents had warned them of this place, saying that none had returned from its heights. They also said it was protected by a ferocious god, who held the form of a bird. 'The Devil's Eye' as it was named was too tempting for them to resist.

After conquering the monstrosity to reach the peak, they rested with ecstasy then lay in the sun. For hours they slept there, absorbing life, creating history.

Out of nowhere a wind so silent rose from its grave, bringing a cool shiver upon the peak of The Devil's Eye. Arithnon became restless. He looked over the village. Normal. His brother, still sleeping in the sunlight, that seemed to have died in power. So why the uneasiness? Why the fear? Why the shadow of a bird which became bigger with every bated breath? Arithnon spun. He tried to scream, then all went dark.

Tom Hawksett (14)
The Mosslands School

Through My Eyes

It was raining slightly, the drizzle running down the windowpane like a tadpole inside a tank, veering apart then gently back together again. Continuous streams of rain fell, splashing into unforgiving puddles on the cold, concrete slabs, which he greeted with a placid smile from the refuge of his old armchair.

He sat and watched the rain all day, watched the clouds turn slowly from grey to black, and the people beneath rushing about with umbrellas like figurines in a spectacular painting. He wondered whether their umbrellas kept them happy or just happier. When they lit the fire at home and warmed up, surrounded by the sure-fire love of their families, would they feel happy or happier? *Love,* he thought, *was a funny old thing.* He would see it deep within the eyes of the people he saw through his window every day, and yet he still thought it ludicrous.

The rain started to ease. He could see a promising ray of sunlight reflecting from a puddle which rippled gently in the passing breeze. One by one, the little people reluctantly edged ambitiously from beneath their umbrellas.

He could see two people alone, standing side by side, in the distance. They stood together, like blackbirds in a forest of discontent, under the asylum of a single umbrella, the copious rain slamming down and deflecting onto the concrete with a splash.

A bolt of thunder pierced through the sky, sending the figurines inside his painting into a restless frenzy. The two figures stood, silently, together, under the umbrella. The moisture rolled down their faces like tears, as they gazed at one another with a transfixed smile.

He smiled.

Love, he thought. *Ludicrous.*

Michael Case-Upton (14)
The Mosslands School

First Meetings Of Lemon Kind

It was just a Sunday morning. Nothing special, just yet another boring day for Kevin to wake up to.

Kevin was an ordinary man, with ordinary-looking features and ordinary brown hair. He went along, doing the same thing he did every morning, when there was an almighty crash.

Kevin jumped up from his breakfast table and ran outside. 'What the hell was tha ...' he began, but stopped as he saw the enormous structure hovering above him. 'This is not going to be one of my good days,' he mumbled.

Suddenly, a great hole opened up in the ship. A single beam of light travelled towards Kevin, and carried him upwards.

'Welcome friend.' Kevin opened his eyes. He was in a circular room, coloured a bright yellow. He jumped to his senses, and realised that he was surrounded by what seemed to be giant lemons.

'Where am I? And what are you?'

'We are currently orbiting Cesar Salad, in the galaxy of the Subway Sandwich,' the head lemon replied. 'We mean you no harm. We are Citronians, and we have brought you here as a guest. Let us give you a tour of the ship.'

'... And this is the escape pod,' said the lemon after a two hour tour of the toilets, 'it's very comfy, try it.'

Kevin stepped into the lemon-shaped pod.

'It even has air conditioning, look.' The lemon pressed a button, and the pod whooshed into space.

'Oops, that was the eject, sorry,' the lemon apologised.

Paul Griffiths-Parry (13)
The Mosslands School

Red Fire

The sun shone through the canopy of towering trees above the detective's head. His face wore the frown of a disgruntled man. He walked briskly across the dusty floor looking at poor, run-down wooden huts either side of him, with desperate looking people staring at him through windows. He managed to hide his inner sympathies - he was not in a good mood.

His mobile jingled and he looked at the screen. It was his captain. He rejected the call instantly. 'Don't wanna know,' he muttered. 'I can't believe they're all back in New York doing proper police work, and I'm in the Gulf of Mexico investigating someone's superstitions about some bird,' he growled quietly to himself. 'Why?'

He had been asked to investigate into the sighting of the mythical Mexican phoenix. A few people had disappeared over the past few months, and many had claimed to have seen a huge red-feathered figure near to the volcano on the island of Mata Muti - in the middle of the Gulf.

He was heading towards the volcano, knowing full-well such suspicions were pointless, and ill-informed. He had no time to investigate petty sightings - so why had his captain assigned him to this pathetic task? Was the captain keeping him in the dark?

The detective was about to turn the next corner, when he heard a noise behind him. He froze. He stood still for a moment. Suddenly, he span round. There was a rush of adrenaline. The burning flames swirled gold and red around a dominant figure in front of him. It was too hot. The image became blurred with every blink. He closed his eyes. He saw red.

Charles Lucking (14)
The Mosslands School

Myth

In the local shop for local people young Dave was buying some sweets. He left the shop and began to turn his usual way when, he heard a crash and a bang. He carried on as he thought it was just a cat but, he then heard a weird noise like nothing he'd heard before. So he crept down the alley to find a bin shivering. He examined the bin and gently lifted the lid.

At first he thought there was nothing there, just a pile of old rubbish, but to his astonishment it turned out to be some sort of alien creature with a long curly neck coming out of a shoe with a head on the end of the neck. Dave jumped back and it jumped out of the bin, it was about to say something when from over the wall jumps another alien but this one looked like a hammer but it was firing a laser at us. The alien jumped up and started hopping away at a tremendous speed. The hammer aimed at Dave, he began to run for his life.

The alien started hopping down the street and people began to scream and some even fainted. The alien hopped down an alley and Dave followed too. They hid behind a bin, the hammer walked down the alley and turned round, it knew they were there. It turned and fired, but the alien picked up a bin lid and it reflected the laser and destroyed the hammer.

Christopher Conlan (14)
The Mosslands School

The Legend Of King Arthur

The climatic battle between King Arthur and the evil Black Knight which brings the famous legend to an end ...

Arthur, king of the Britons, raises his mystical sword, Excalibur, defensively over his head; easily parrying a strike from the evil Black Knight. Taking a step back and bringing his sword round, Arthur throws a wild attack at the Black Knight knowing that it wouldn't hit its mark. The Black Knight parried Excalibur, and took a step back, preparing to strike; and to kill.

The Black Knight moved his sword and sliced it into Arthur's stomach.

Arthur collapsed. He felt the sword pierce his armour and crash through his flesh. The end of the sword reappeared through his back.

The Black Knight pulled his sword out of the King's body. 'At last, I am King,' the Black Knight muttered before turning round to walk away.

Arthur slumped forward, feeling the blade leave his body. He knew he was about to die. He knew he had failed everyone. An image of a sword in a stone filled his mind, and sudden determination filled him. Arthur rose to meet the Black Knight's challenge.

Swinging his blade in a wide arc, Arthur brought Excalibur across the knight's sword arm, tearing it from the knight's body. Then, Arthur knocked him down. The Black Knight frantically reached for his dagger. Arthur raised Excalibur high above his head, 'Now you die!' he managed to say before tearing the knight's head from his body. Smiling, Arthur didn't notice the dagger sticking out of his chest. He slumped to one side. Leaning on Excalibur, Arthur died.

Chris Chamberlain (14)
The Mosslands School